tell everything

tell everything
SALLY COOPER

THE DUNDURN GROUP
TORONTO

Editor: Barry Jowett
Copy-editor: Andrea Waters
Design: Alison Carr
Printer: Marquis

Library and Archives Canada Cataloguing in Publication

Cooper, Sally (Sally Elizabeth)
  Tell everything / Sally Cooper.

ISBN 978-1-55002-775-4

  I. Title.

PS8555.O59228T44 2007   C813'.6   C2007-904681-9

1   2   3   4   5   11   10   09   08   07

Conseil des Arts   Canada Council
du Canada   for the Arts

ONTARIO ARTS COUNCIL
CONSEIL DES ARTS DE L'ONTARIO

We acknowledge the support of **The Canada Council for the Arts** and the **Ontario Arts Council** for our publishing program. We also acknowledge the financial support of the **Government of Canada** through the **Book Publishing Industry Development Program** and **The Association for the Export of Canadian Books**, and the **Government of Ontario** through the **Ontario Book Publishers Tax Credit** program, and the **Ontario Media Development Corporation**.

Care has been taken to trace the ownership of copyright material used in this book. The author and the publisher welcome any information enabling them to rectify any references or credits in subsequent editions.

J. Kirk Howard, President

Printed and bound in Canada.
Printed on recycled paper.

www.dundurn.com

Dundurn Press	Gazelle Book Services Limited	Dundurn Press
3 Church Street, Suite 500	White Cross Mills	2250 Military Road
Toronto, Ontario, Canada	High Town, Lancaster, England	Tonawanda, NY
M5E 1M2	LA1 4XS	U.S.A. 14150

for Daniel

Give me your skin
as sheer as a cobweb
let me open it up
and listen in and scoop out the dark

"Rapunzel"
Anne Sexton

My mother told me a story once about a foolish princess. We were hiking up the path to Banana Rock. Sunlight slanted through the branches. She made up the story, and I held her hand and matched my steps to hers. The princess was vain and not very pretty. When an old baron asked to marry her, her mother celebrated. The baron called the princess beautiful. She believed him and fell in love. The night before the wedding, the baron invited her to his house. Her mother insisted she wear a veil until she'd sealed the union. But the princess wanted her fiancé to admire her. When the princess walked into a hall of mirrors inside the castle, she threw off the veil and found herself in a dungeon packed with demon brides. A sorcerer turned her into a toothless old woman with a smelly, aching body. Because the princess was vain, the sorcerer made her sit in the hall of mirrors, where her ugly image stretched out in every direction. She warned each of the baron's new brides-to-be not to look at herself, but none would listen. Even her mother said she'd be better off dead. "It's not my fault," cried my mother in the foolish princess's voice. Her own voice rang with a smug glee that meant she thought it really was.

My mother took short steps and looked down at me while she talked. As she told her story her hand heated up, though it stayed dry. Her voice flared too, then got thin, flowery. I could hear how much the princess wanted to be beautiful and loved. I heard how silly she was, and how doomed. The story got me angry, and I kicked at the sand. At Banana Rock we took off our sandals and wiggled our toes in the sun. I cried a little and threw stones into the pool below. My mother took my chin in her free hand and said, "Don't worry. One day a smart girl comes along who doesn't need a mirror or a prince to know how beautiful she is. The crone becomes young again and escapes with her beautiful new friend." My mother pulled me into her lap, even though I was getting too big for it. Then we climbed down to wade in the water and the story left me until long after my mother was gone.

chapter 1

I woke up hot. My eyes burned. Images of cellar windows, angled light faded into joy. I pulled the duvet over my head and tucked in my feet.

"Kiss me so I can go to work," Alex said. He stood over me in his trench coat, two plums clutched to his chest. I lifted my head off the pillow, eyes shut, and we pressed lips.

In June, after we'd graduated, Alex and I had rented the bungalow on Shelby Street. Flats Mills had a Lucky Dollar, a diner, two churches, and a strip of antique and craft shops. Beyond the town sat hundred-acre fields of corn, potatoes, soy, and sod. The land moved higher to the north, and in certain darknesses its hills gave a view of Toronto lit-up, an hour away. We'd got what we wanted. Country and city. Space and each other.

We painted the living room Chimayo red and hung it with nudes. Some originals, some prints. Nobody dropped by, nobody had our phone number. Living here felt like an escape trick.

"I'm bushed," I said.

"You screamed last night. And punched me once." He sat on my feet. Images of wet hands, a dripping mattress seeped into me.

"I do that sometimes." I stroked the sheet.

"Nightmares are hot. And I get to do the protective guy thing." He swelled his chest and sucked in his cheeks.

I scratched his beard where the skin was peeling underneath. Last night Alex had hugged me as we walked around Flats Mills inhaling our skunky weed and our neighbours' sweet maple firesmoke. We'd shared a pocket and a glove and talked about his internship at St. Mary's Hospital. He'd called me his girl and said he'd buy us a farmhouse once he set up his practice. I liked his love, though it felt simple, finite. My own, lesser love dwelled on his staying and left it at that. I'd clutched his cuff and called him "Sweetness" to stop myself from showing him anyone but the person he knew he loved.

"You'd be surprised what I know, my dear."

I found Alex's statements cryptic, but they had their appeal. They kept us from talking about what made us uncomfortable. We never said "I love you" or discussed what our love felt like and what it meant to us, and we didn't talk about marriage or children or why he gave up art for medicine. Cozy, we stayed hopeful.

"What do you know?"

"Everything is good between us, and we made a good choice coming here."

"Any choice we made would have worked."

"But we made this one and we're happy."

"We are happy," I said.

He got up, and the nerves in my feet sputtered. Then he was leaving — shutting off the stereo, rattling keys, closing doors. The hatchback's engine turned over with a screech, tires swashed puddles, and the house fell silent.

I called Vangie and said I had a migraine.

"The flashes and bangs stopped an hour ago. I'm taking a

break. Next comes the weeping and vomiting."

"Make sure you have plenty of tissues, dear," she said.

"It's the season. You know —" I said, ready to talk, but Vangie had an interview and had to go.

Vangie was the head editor at InfoText. She had her own office and suffered from migraines, so I let her think I did, too. Once, I drove her to Emergency at ten in the morning. I had to pull over three times so she could throw up. The hospital gave her a shot and she slept for two days. Afterward, discomfited, she took me to dinner and I consoled her with a false list of my own symptoms. I liked the closeness, the shared burden. At InfoText, I sat in a cubicle cluster with five other grunts entering data. On a good week, I could do a whole book.

Afternoons I watched talk shows until Alex got back from the hospital. Whenever I brought up serial killers, Alex said, "Why do you want to glorify those losers?"

"Good point," I said. "But successful couples keep some separate interests. All the magazines say so."

"Why not get a more useful hobby, then? Make us a toilet paper doll. A driftwood centrepiece. A Popsicle stick lamp."

"Because then you'd want to join me."

Sometimes I worked on the outline of my novel about a sculptor who'd made a box that conjured up the ghost of a run-away slave. Mostly I built the box, so I'd know what to say about it when I was ready to write. It took up most of the second bedroom.

The box — my character's box — tapered like a cone and had six sides made of chicken wire, foam rubber, and canvas. It could hold one person, two in a pinch. It needed a door, though, with a lock. I planned to use brass.

After a bath, I wrapped myself in towels and did a slow air-dry in front of *The Heidi Roth-Lopez Show*. Heidi, a former alco-holic soap opera teen, hectored a forty-five-year-old man en-gaged to a seventeen-year-old girl who'd gone to the same school as his sons. The sons scowled from the audience. The girlfriend sat behind them, in her eyes an animal sheen. She looked caught, sore, her tight mouth ungiving. The man's eyes were clear pools of unexpected, inane light.

Heidi emphasized key words in her questions then turned her sly gaze on the audience, who shouted "Perv!" and "Sickie!" at the father, the girl, even the sons. Throughout, the man looked lusty and contrite, the girl ready to bolt, yet their stories had a veneer of joy and rightness that aroused in me a quizzical respect. Clearly, they relished the spectacle as the holes inside them gaped for all to see.

I turned the TV off, got dressed, and fastened my hair with a barrette shaped like a fish. In the foyer I double-knotted my boot laces and buttoned a trench coat against the dripping fog.

Head down, I fixed my gaze on the road. Corroded leaves rimmed the ditch. I stretched out my sweater neck, the air warm despite the damp. I stepped around potholes and puddles. Gravel and mud packed the grooves of my soles.

I walked the half block to Queen Street, past Sandy White Woolens and Beard of Bees Crafts, open weekends only. Tires slapped the wet asphalt. I crossed to the post office. The mail contained a hydro bill and a flyer for Drainy Days Plumbing. Only one letter had come for me since we moved here, from Jenna, my first-year roommate, who taught in Czechoslovakia. None of my friends lived close.

I passed the Cannonball Diner with its smoke and oil pong then ducked into the Lucky Dollar for a paper. The tabloids didn't come in until Tuesday, so I got the *Toronto Telstar*. Outside, I checked out the front page. Yet another offensive headline: "Lawyer dead, wife nailed." Beside it walked a tanned woman in a pink turtleneck and jean jacket flanked by two police. My breath cinched and I sank into a crouch, back against the ice freezer, the paper on my knees.

At twelve, I wrote my first story about a homicidal mother. I wrote more at thirteen, fourteen, and fifteen, right up until I moved to Cloud Lake. I typed the stories fast and made them bloody, amoral. In each one the mother swings her hair and looks over her shoulder the way my mother did the day she drove off with the man she met at the Dominion Hotel.

When he read them, Alex rubbed my earlobes and said, "It's always the same story with you, Pauline," and he was right. Only this one, I hadn't made up. I knew the victim and I knew the killer. The accused. The woman on the front page. The police had arrested her because they believed she'd murdered her husband.

Fog buried the treetops and swathed the Bethany United Church steeple. Even under arrest, Ramona Hawkes wrapped confidence around sickness and fear. She'd gained weight. It was hard to see specifics, but I did check, then, ashamed, dug at my ear and scanned the highlights. She'd stabbed him — *someone* had stabbed him — thirty-one times. She was stronger than I remembered. But that was wrong. She had been strong. I remembered her strong.

In my office I dropped the *Telstar* on the floor. Ramona stared past me. Alex would comment on her body, compare it unfavourably to mine. I didn't want to hear it. I placed the folded paper face down in the slave box and picked up some sandpaper. As I tried to block out James Hawkes and his wife, I ended up thinking about the profound connection between killer and victim. I missed my shows and didn't hear Alex as I rubbed the brass to the smoothness of old skin.

That was October 1990. One cold morning the following summer, I lay wrapped in towels on the couch watching Heidi Roth-Lopez interview the mother of a giant baby. The baby sat in a separate room with a camera trained on him. A screen behind Heidi and the parents showed the baby to the audience. He had floppy legs and a wet, vapid face. His eyes were smart and dazzling, slightly drugged. The audience tutted and moaned. Someone yelled, "Freak!" I wanted him to be real as much as I didn't. Maybe more. The mother wanted it, too, and I admired her show of helpless need. Shellacked with tears, she exposed the space in her the size of a fat, diapered teenager. I'd quit data entry by then and was collecting unemployment insurance and trying to write.

When the knocking started, I muted the TV and crouch-walked to the window, dropping towels. Two people in wind-breakers stood on the stoop, their faces blocked by the awning. A cop car nosed my Hustler's tail.

"Answer the door please, Ms. Brown," a woman's voice called. "It's the police."

I haven't done anything. What about Alex? I don't want to know. I skittered into the bedroom and got under the covers.

"Pauline Elizabeth Brown?" a man's voice asked through the screen. I'd left the bedroom window open.

"Yes."

"Let us in, please. You've already got two neighbours hang-ing over the fence. Or we'll climb in through here. Suit yourself."

I tugged the curtains across and crawled to the dresser. I had no clean underwear, so I put on a one-piece bathing suit under an Indian print skirt. By the time I opened the door I had goosebumps. The damp suit smelled of chlorine. The cops stepped into the foyer.

"I'm Detective Debra Young and this is Detective Wayne Stanton. We understand you used to live in Cloud Lake."

Detective Stanton was black-eyed and tall with a mean-wise smile that poked into one cheek. Detective Young had pink cheeks and a severe blonde ponytail. They held open leather wallets with gold badges on one side and photo IDs on the other.

"What's the problem?" Behind them, the empty street looked expectant, prying.

"We need you to confirm that you lived in Cloud Lake, in Brampton." Detective Young's voice had a pleasant gloss that strove to make you like her even as she extracted something dear.

"That's right. I did."

"Good. Did you know Ramona Hawkes?"

Cornered, I croaked a yes, with dread and relief. The *Telstar* with Ramona's picture sat in my box, but I hadn't read about her since that day. I'd avoided the news, too. Without details, my mind had offered flashes of pores, stubble, and knuckles — my body greased with a smell that brought me up to three baths a day. I snapped the bathing suit strap and agreed to let them drive me to the station.

"Ramona Hawkes is accused of a Peel County murder," Detective Young explained over her shoulder as we headed up Highway 400. Her ponytail draped over the headrest. I studied the handle-free doors. I used to know a guy, Dave Watson, who'd busted free of a cop car by kicking the window out with his feet. "But the South Simcoe station is closer to your house, only ten minutes away. We'd rather talk to you on your own turf." Suddenly I had a turf. I felt like pawing it.

The air smelled of corn. "Tornado ripped through here a few years back," Detective Stanton said. "You can see the damage if you know where to look." We were driving past a break in the trees where the brush lay flat.

They took me to a room with a scarred table and four chairs. Detective Young fiddled with the blind so it blocked the sun and a blue patch of Lake Simcoe then sat at the end. She was tall, and her knee hit the table when she crossed her legs.

"You're late-breaking," Detective Stanton said. He spoke with relieved glee, as if he'd expected I'd give him more trouble. "We didn't know about you until after Ramona Hawkes's preliminary hearing."

"How did you find me?" Maybe Ramona had given them my name. I tugged each finger away from its socket.

Detective Stanton looked at Detective Young, who twitched. He leaned an elbow on the table as if he wanted to share a secret, his body poised in the relaxed coil of a practised flirt. His wedding band caught the light like treasure.

"You weren't in her yearbook, that's obvious. She had letters and scripts. Your name turned up."

"Scripts?"

"Scripts with your name on them. It appears you wrote them. Keep in mind your statement could help convict Ramona Hawkes at the trial. Smoke?"

I took one and let him light it. After an easy drag, I tapped the cigarette against the crimp-edged ashtray then held it away from my body. The scripts I remembered, but I couldn't think of what letters I'd written. I wanted to help but didn't see how I could.

"How will talking to me make a difference? I knew her five years ago. I have no idea why — or if — she did it. I haven't followed the story at all."

"What happened at the prelim is public domain," Stanton said. He hitched the back of his pants with one hand. Young inspected her nails, cut blunt and left bare, then spoke. "You might want to bone up further at the library, but we can give you the basics." She had the soothing voice of a shill, and I quickened, alert for loopholes.

"There is evidence that Ramona and James Hawkes drugged and assaulted teenage girls. While Ramona Hawkes is not on trial here for sexual assault, at issue is whether her husband forced her to participate and she killed him out of fear for her own life, or whether she shared her husband's proclivities and killed him out of jealousy over someone else."

She twirled the words "someone else" into a question, as if she had an idea of the other woman's identity but wanted to see how I responded. After all, Ramona had kept my scripts. I must have meant something to her. Maybe she envied me all these years later. If so, I didn't want to know. Let another friend carry that burden.

"We're going back to establish patterns, digging up what we can. Every small detail could help."

"Whose side are you on?" I asked.

"It isn't about sides, Pauline. We work for the Crown."

"So you think she did it?"

"There is enough evidence to go to trial, yes."

"We'd like you to tell us whatever you remember about the times you spent at the Hawkeses' house," Stanton said. "What you saw and heard, whatever you observed, however small."

"But I didn't know them long."

"We have one witness who knew them less than a week. Your story has merit. We'd like to hear it."

"How about some pop? A coffee?" Palms on the table, Detective Young shifted her weight as if to stand. She had a precise assurance that spoke of no disappointments. A leader. A prizewinning girl.

I brought the cigarette to my mouth. Ashes rose then settled on my skirt. These two had the main events figured. I'd have to give them details, tell them what I guessed they already knew.

"Shall we?"

"Okay." I tucked my hands into my armpits. "But go easy on me. I'm nervous. It's hard to talk about this kind of thing."

"We understand. We'll take it slow, then," said Detective Young. "As slow as you like."

"How did you meet Ramona?" Detective Stanton asked. "Give us times and dates."

"I knew her a year," I said. "Him less than that. I met them in 1985." I took care not to say either name.

Detective Stanton asked about touching. Sex.

"What? Will I have to testify? I don't want —"

"Possibly," said Detective Young. "Though I'm afraid you don't have a choice, if it comes to that. What is it?"

"This is embarrassing. I hardly knew this woman and I don't remember much. My husband doesn't even know."

"I'm sorry," said Detective Young. "Maybe you'll want to speak someone about that?"

"Isn't that what I'm doing?" I reined in my smile so they wouldn't take me for a smartass. I wanted to leave but I had no way to get home.

"A professional, I was thinking. A counsellor. We can give

you some names, if you like. So you know, we do sometimes use the statement, no witness. The trial starts in March. Please, your story's important. Tell us every detail. Don't lie or guess. Wayne will take notes, and I'll tape you."

Someone else would come forward. Another friend. They wouldn't need my story to get a conviction. Girls, he'd said. There were others. Even if I was the other woman in Ramona's mind, I didn't need to be in theirs. I talked for almost an hour then stopped.

"I don't remember any more," I said, and I didn't, not really. I hadn't for a long time.

The house reeled, too bright, nothing in its expected place. My body felt wrong, far away and not my own. After the detectives dropped me off, I stood inside the door and held out my hands. I touched my fingers as if I'd never seen fingers before. In the living room I stared at the nudes. Not one looked back at me, the faces haircurtained, buried in armpits, turned away, or cut from the frame.

Until I saw her photo in the *Telstar*, I'd forgotten Ramona. I never thought about what happened and I never talked about it. Today, I'd rewarded the detectives' questions. They'd picked at the details and prodded until I told more than I'd bargained. The cops had my statement now. I'd signed it so they could read it in court and I wouldn't have to appear. Since Alex didn't follow murder trials, he needn't find out. I could stay the same in his eyes. I could forget again.

In my office, I kneeled in front of the box and turned the *Telstar* over. Ramona had worn Ray-Bans for her arrest, and a pink turtleneck. She'd rounded out, but little else had changed in five years. I brought the paper to my desk. My novel outline had hit a hundred pages. The novel needed scenes. I tackled one in which the ghost watches the sculptor with her lover. Soon I switched to my stack of character cards. I crossed out the sculptor's description and wrote "blonde." Then "Ramona." I scribbled over the card and shredded it. Cards were stupid and they weren't writing. I shut off my computer and grabbed a notepad. With the *Telstar* on my knee, I leaned against the box and wrote. I wrote what I saw and what I thought and what I might have thought. Some of the places changed, our names, too. I put Ramona's side in, but writing it made me uncomfortable and I didn't think I would do it again.

The first time Peck saw her, Mona was applying lip gloss in the parking lot of the Rodeo strip mall. Peck was seventeen, had moved to Westwoods three weeks earlier, and was sticking Velcroed poker chips to the New Releases shelf near the window of Venus Video when she saw this woman in a black leather mini and a pink ripped T-shirt with the word "City" across the front in script. The woman had long platinum hair and wore a police cap and frilly anklets inside white leather pumps like the ladies in the ZZ Top videos. She stood on the asphalt in the "Reserved for Venus Video" spot. Her perfectness bugged Peck. Her phoniness. She looked like nobody Peck had ever seen close up, not in Kashag and certainly not here, and Peck couldn't stop staring at her, trying to break the whole into pieces she could understand. She applied the lip gloss so slowly, dabbing the fuzzy end of the applicator on her puckered lips, dipping the stick in the pink container, swiping it back and forth, loading each lip with oily goo. Peck could imagine the candy smell. The Vaseline taste. The lip gloss irked her.

At the time Peck saw her applying the pink lip gloss at the Rodeo strip mall, Mona lived with Jim Hawkes at 17 Covered Wagon Trail in a detached home that backed onto a field. She had met Jim the previous Christmas at a law school pub she'd gone to with Larry Buxton, her Man & Society teacher. She went home with Jim and never left. She worked as one of three legal secretaries at the small firm of Henderson, Albert & Tizz. A picture of her Rottweiler, Albert, sat in a brass frame on her desk. The Rotty wore a blue kerchief and stood splay-legged and smiling on Wasaga Beach, an orange KONG at his feet. Jim had a dog allergy so Albert lived with her parents in the Smythefield subdivision west of Main Street and north of Buyers World mall. Mona liked the fields behind 17 Covered Wagon Trail. She liked squinting at the light on the pond water and hearing the cracked sounds of the ducks. Smythefield had no open spaces. It had older and taller trees. She liked being the only one walking the streets in no shade. She liked the sameness of the houses. By June 1985, she was engaged. She was planning her wedding. She had girlfriends both older and younger than seventeen. She liked a good caper and was impressed when she walked into Venus Video and Peck Brown was watching Bonnie and Clyde.

chapter 2

The summer Peck was nine, her mother ran away with another man. Peck was playing with Malcolm Salter next door when his mom brought her a can of root beer and said, "Go home now. Your dad wants you."

That night, and for many nights afterward, she felt dead, as if her mother had murdered her.

In the years that followed, she read the paperbacks about the Black Donnellys and Jack the Ripper her mom had left in the bathroom. With her mom's card, Peck signed murder books out of the Kashag Public Library. She looked at the victims before their deaths, the women in headscarves and sunglasses, the men in suits with skinny ties, and she looked at the killers' hooded eyes and beat-down faces in their mug shots. Sometimes she looked at the bodies and their dumping grounds. Bodies on couches or beds, in ditches or fields. Some books blanked out the corpses. Others showed autopsy photos with pulpy mouths, glassy stares, bloodsmears.

She imagined her mom killing her. She pictured her body stuffed in the rocks, her mom's thumbprints bruised into her throat. When the police lifted her up, maggots would drop off. The police would gag at the smell. Then they'd put her mom in jail. Faced with the autopsy photos, her mom would say, "Shoot, she was prettier when I knew her."

Her mom was Margery Virginia and she was Pauline Elizabeth and her dad was Harold Ray Brown. Nobody called him Harold — nor Harry, a name for a rounder, balder man. He was Hank. When other men said it, especially when drinking, it came out like a swear. Sometimes it sounded like Hunk. She pictured him as a side of meat, rosy brown and slimy. He called her Peck for the hard kisses she gave. She liked to call him Heck. Heck no, it's not a bother. What the heck. I'm gonna give you heck. A watered-down cuss. A non-word. She liked that Heck rhymed with Peck.

One fall during moose season, Malcolm Salter from next door came into her kitchen swinging a plastic bag.

"Want to see?" he said, and Peck said, "Sure."

Grinning, he displayed a moose heart with veins and tubes and fat. One whiff of iron blood and she kicked him. Malcolm snatched the bag away and kicked her back.

She helped Hank do the tanning. They mashed the brains into a paste over a fire. He staked the hide on racks behind the shed, and she worked it soft with a stick.

One time Hank presented her with a deerskin purse, from his first. "She stood out like sawdust against the snow," he said. Peck pictured the bullet hitting the doe's glowing heart and a cooked venison roast revealed in a burst of wood shavings. "I had this made for your mother, but she left it behind. Might be she wanted you to have it." He spoke with a strangled cheeriness. Stiff, she watched him hang the strap from her shoulder, his features receding as if washed out by sudden, heavy rain. The purse moved like cloth and had a stubbly nap Peck liked to brush against her skin. She stored it under her bed with her mom's library card and feathered clip inside.

At twelve she wrote her first story. Her characters laughed and swung their Cher hair as they killed whole families in inventive, domestic ways. They always got caught, though, and not by their daughters, either.

Peck stopped talking about her mom, but Hank didn't. He told stories about Margery as if they'd had coffee that morning. If she ever came back, Peck figured he'd yield like worked skin.

In June 1980, five years before they moved to Westwoods, Hank turned thirty-five. Peck was twelve. The morning of his birthday, she caught her orderly father standing in the kitchen in boxers and a vest. A gob of shaving foam trailed along his jaw as he tilted his head back and poured a stream of milk down his throat. Other changes followed. He came home earlier from his horseshoe tourneys and what he called his "Poke Her" nights. He mentioned Margery less and limited himself to one girlfriend, a twenty-one-year-old horsewoman named Sue Smedley. And he started the plan. The plan he said would give them something to show for their lives. The plan that meant moving. He applied to more than a hundred companies and pored over MLS catalogues with house listings north and west of Toronto. He would get a good job and set up a life far from his friends. From Kashag. Peck could only watch as Hank grew up.

By the time they moved south, Hank had worked there for four years, at Apco Moulding running a machine that made margarine tubs. He drove the two hours and change each way and took twelve-hour shifts, three nights on, two days off; four nights on, three days off; sometimes seven and seven.

Peck's chief impression of this period was Hank collapsed stubble-cheeked on the couch, tan boots lolling, sock bottoms black, coveralls faded airplane grey with musky grease stains. Measured snores replaced the ripping songs that used to follow his benders.

When he was upright between shifts after a sixteen-hour

sleep and a shave, his smile had a new quality, and he held Peck in his gaze. He acted proud and on the verge of a promise. Peck hated him then, but she had no right. He was throwing their lives through this upheaval to give her a better future, but she worried that one day she might look up from her murder stories and find he, too, had stepped out for good.

Malcolm Salter grew tall and hard-shouldered the summer before Peck left for Westwoods. They took to playing Monopoly in the Salters' trailer and talking about the Beatles. Peck had fallen in love with Paul McCartney after she'd found out he was fourteen when his mother died of cancer. John Lennon had seen his mother get hit by a streetcar, but he had Aunt Mimi. Whom did Paul have? She didn't tell Malcolm that she wrote letters to Paul or that she wrote Paul's replies. In the letters, Paul called her "my love" and told her maybe he was amazed. She would go to Scotland and work as a nanny at the McCartney sheep farm, and Paul would love her and Linda would bow out. She believed in the goodness of Linda.

One day, at the end of a treatise on the backward looping of "Strawberry Fields Forever," Malcolm straightened his money piles. They'd turned on the lamps and closed the curtains against the sun. He picked at the vinyl piping on a cushion.

"Let's go into the house," he said. "I'll show you my *Beatlemags.*"

She scooped up four houses and placed a hotel on Indiana Avenue and said, "As long as we come back to this game."

Inside the door, one set of stairs led up to the kitchen and another to a curtained-off area of the basement. Malcolm had taped a collage of Beatles pictures to the unpainted drywall.

Malcolm fetched two cans of beer and put on *Abbey Road.* He offered her a *Beatlemag* then disappeared upstairs. Unconcerned, Peck read a column about real-life Beatle encounters. She planned to submit her Paul letters.

Malcolm dropped back on the couch, crossed his legs, jiggled his foot. He reached an arm up, then dropped it to his side. "Come upstairs," he said. "The rentals are out." Malcolm's

parents spent their days fishing at Twelve Mile Lake. His father was a retired police officer known as the Sergeant.

"Like Sergeant Pepper," Peck had said.

"But not as cool."

Malcolm scorned sports and the outdoors. He said it disgusted the Sergeant that he wouldn't make a military man, let
alone a cop.

Under the bathroom sink, Malcolm displayed a stack of
crimped *Penthouses* and *Hustlers*. Peck told him about the toilet
reading material her mother had left behind and said, "I guess
that's the difference between my house and yours."

"Not necessarily," Malcolm said. He took her to his brother
Mike's room and handed her a binder. The plastic sleeves held
photographs of murder scenes. There were women strangled by
pantyhose, bras, or ties and men shot in the back of the head or
the chest, and there was much dismemberment. A brain blown
out of a victim's skull and lying at his feet. A severed head sitting on railroad tracks. A woman with her head on her lap. A
woman's limbless torso. Bodies burned, stabbed, mangled, shot.
Malcolm cocked his head as she turned the pages and thumbed
the plastic.

"The Sergeant collected these. He gave them to my brother
when he got on the force."

"Imagine what you'll get if you become a cop."

"We'll never know."

The pattern of their afternoons changed. After passing Go
five times each, they sat on Mike's bed, the carnage album on
their laps. Malcolm told the story of each photo, the crime,
where and when it happened, what the police figured out.
Sometimes they analyzed the bodies in the *Hustler* spreads, but
they preferred the corpses. Malcolm delivered his comments on
the nude models and the crime scenes in the same measured,
baffled tone he used when detailing the Beatles' recording techniques or informing her she owed him $90 for landing on St.
James Place with one house. She opened her mouth and closed
her eyes in a show of shock and disgust, though her library true

crimes had plenty of photos, and (something she wouldn't tell Malcolm) a *Hustler* lived under the sink at her home, too.

At school, they developed a set of greetings based on Beatles songs. Her favourite was Sergeant Salter's Lonely Hearts Club Son. He liked Strawberry Peck Forever.

The day before she moved to Westwoods, Peck found Malcolm on the trailer couch reading *Mad*.

"Polythene Peck."

"Back in the U.S.S. Malcolm."

"Peck Came in Through the Bathroom Window."

"Nowhere Malcolm."

She sat on the sink and asked, "How's the Sergeant?"

"They released the boat two weeks ago. Let the game begin." Malcolm tossed the *Mad* aside and swung up.

"I don't have time for Monopoly, Malcolm. We're going tomorrow. My dad's moving stuff today."

"Okay."

"We could do other things. What we usually do. What about the *Beatlemags*?"

His head knocked the skylight handle. His thighs in jeans brushed her bare knees. She stayed put. He propped one hand on the stove and the other on the sink and kissed her without asking. She found his tongue and sucked it.

He recoiled. "Where'd you learn that?"

Saliva dried on her cheeks. She'd never kissed with her mouth open before.

He wiped his lips and cupped her head. "I didn't mean it," he said. "It's an asshole guy thing to say. What a guy who reads *Hustler* would say."

"Mean Mr. Malcolm."

"A Hard Day's Peck."

He lifted her onto the couch, where they wrestled and ribtickled then settled into an unbroken kiss. Her tongue met his, and she gave herself over to the sun cradling her neck and the cushions' dry-vinyl crackle.

"I am moving tomorrow," she said after a while.

"I know. That's what makes this okay."

"It wouldn't be if I weren't?"

"It would be better. But we'd be playing Monopoly right now if you weren't."

His damp armpit curved around her cheek. She breathed his cottony T-shirt heat.

"We won't write each other or anything, will we?"

"Give me your address. I may show up someday." He kissed her bangs. "Just don't off anybody without me."

"Bang Bang Malcolm's Silver Hammer —"

"— came down upon Peck's head!"

They didn't kiss again.

On June 7, 1985, Hank strapped their beds, dressers, and suitcases to the Ranger and drove Peck to their new house on Hartley Horse Way in Westwoods, a new development in north Brampton. She carried *The Black Donnellys*, the feathered clip, her mom's library card, and the McCartney letters in her mom's deerskin purse.

They arrived at Westwoods late Sunday morning under a yellow sky. Number 39 looked the same as the others, a two-storey semi-detached with a garage. It had two small windows upstairs and one medium down. It had no shutters or any other decorations. The bricks were rusty pink and the trim off-white. Steep concrete stairs led to the front door. Three evergreen shrubs squatted under the front window, and a spindly tree with pointy leaves graced the end of the driveway. No tree on Hartley Horse Way reached higher than the roof peaks, and there was little shade.

They entered through the garage, which smelled like potatoes. Hank had arranged the living room the same as in Kashag. Above the couch hung the gun rack adorned with photos of two does suspended by their hind hooves from winter branches. Saloon doors took her into the kitchen, set up like home. The red table and yellow chairs below the sunburst clock. Mrs. Salter's lemon squares in a Tupperware container on the counter. Sue Smedley's thoroughbred calendar on the fridge. Only Burt was missing. Dogs didn't belong in subdivisions, claimed Hank, so the Salters had kept him. The dog was in his prime, and Hank intended to hunt him that year.

Hank banned her from her bedroom until he had it ready. She helped him move the furniture into the hall. Then he showed her the cable box. She punched buttons and ended up watching a woman in a long dress strolling through a park singing, "He walks with us, he talks with us."

After an hour or so, Hank called her down the hall. "This is it, baby," he said. "This is your new life."

He stepped aside and nudged her. She didn't dare turn back and show him that although she loved him and wanted to feel as happy as he did, this room with its white walls and its high square window made her think not of her future, but of her mom. Her new room, her Beatles poster pinned above her dresser like at home, was not her new life, but a reminder of what had irretrievably gone.

chapter 3

In February, I was making blueberry pancakes when cops visited our house again. Alex shovelled the driveway while I stood on the stoop in my slippers. An officer confirmed my name and wrote down my occupation as unemployed. He handed me a subpoena then drove off.

I dropped the sheet on the kitchen table. New butter sizzled straight to brown, the element too high. I tossed the frying pan into the sink and slammed another onto a cold burner. Stanton had lied. And the other one, Young — crafty blonde. Weekends were supposed to be sacred. They couldn't make me testify. What happened had nothing to do with our lives now, I'd tell Alex, and trust him not to hold a grudge. Snow clods rattled the window. Untroubled, he'd stayed outside. I didn't like to let him down.

He came in fifteen minutes later, his hair chaotic from his toque.

"Allo, luv," he said. He was in a British mood.

"Sweetness."

We ate on the living room couch.

"When that bobby pulled up, I buckled and surrendered you."

"Snitch."

"Fugitive."

Since I'd quit my job at InfoText, I'd taken to letting the phone ring. Whenever the detectives or the Crown called, I deleted their messages. *Come and get me.* I liked the image of myself as a runaway — its reckless mystery, and its privacy — though I doubted I'd have the nerve. Ramona's trial started next month.

"It's a trial they're asking me to testify at. No big deal." *Good. Minimize it.*

"You say that like it's a birthday party. How could this happen? You don't know anybody. Is it your dad?"

"Nobody you know."

"Then it is your dad. Seriously, why haven't you told me?"

"You don't like it when I talk murder."

His eyes churned bark-grey. "You know a murderer?"

"Murderess. Accused. And not know. Knew."

We read the subpoena together. The Queen commanded me to report to District Court on Wednesday, April 22.

My voice tinny, I told him that Ramona had befriended me in high school, when my dad and I moved south from Haliburton to Cloud Lake, a Brampton subdivision, that we hit it off in the summer but drifted apart once school started. "Ramona had a career and a house and a fiancé. I lived with my dad and went to high school," I said. I left out my panic, how my tongue roped at saying "Ramona."

"They must need you as a character witness," he said. Trustful, assessing, he took me at my word. How could I forget? My part in the trial he would see as a part-time job, a duty that occupied but didn't own me. He wouldn't make the leaps, connect this to that, invent causes or blame.

"It's for the Crown, not the defence. I talked to the cops last summer. I thought they wouldn't need me for the trial, but they called last week."

I settled my hands against his. We pushed our palms until our fingers bent and our knuckles cracked.

"Did you end on bad terms?"

"We ended. She got married and I left for university. Then I met you."

Alex had said "I love you" first and quickly. We were in his dad's BMW with the sunroof open. Drunk on whisky, I was making noises and rocking into him. He was the first man I'd had inside me. We were parked by the sea a thousand miles east on what we'd convinced his parents was a painting excursion. I was nineteen.

He didn't repeat the words. Afterward, I lay under a blanket and shot back more whisky.

"What did you say?"

"When?"

"Then. There."

"You heard me."

"I heard something but I'm not sure."

"You heard."

"What I heard was something a person would want to say again."

"Re-ally."

"Maybe it's not what I thought."

"Maybe it is and I don't want to say."

"It's okay to say."

"I know."

The air was pearling up as we stuck our feet into desert boots then stepped onto wet sand littered with shell fragments and spread with sticky seaweed.

"We should move higher. The tide."

We drove to grass and pitched a pup tent between the car and the ocean. I crawled into the sleeping bag as the nylon filtered pinkish orange light. Alex tied the flaps, zipped the screen. He got in beside me, and I pulled off my jeans now that I had his warm legs. I wouldn't let him see me upright without clothes. Later, I wouldn't sleep in the same bed at other people's houses. We tangled together, legs and arms, heart against heart, and he said it again, once, before I slipped into drunken slumber, and I heard it and remembered, and from then on he felt okay saying it and we could talk about it.

I didn't remember beginning to love him. He built love around me, and I sat inside. I had known him the same as I'd known anyone else. Then something shifted. He named it, and I lingered long enough so all that mattered was staying there. In bed, beside him, I'd catalogue our body parts. His slimmer hips and ankles, our same-sized hands. The few inches he had on me, though neither of us was tall. At the thought of him leaving, my longing throbbed.

Back in Guelph, Alex moved into my room. Soon we had our own apartment overlooking the Speed River. We sealed our love in a ceremony with candles and body painting and acid. We spoke vows and played Hendrix's "… And the Gods Made Love" as everything reduced to vibrating particles.

We found the rings at the farmers' market, two entwined snakes, heads meeting. The rings made us husband and wife. I'd used Shore as my last name ever since.

"It's not about marriage," he said as we walked along Macdonell Street to the Albion Hotel for fries and a pitcher of draught.

"You don't believe in it?"

"It's a convention. What we have is no less valid because we didn't say the prescribed words and get the paperwork. It's what we make it. Nobody can take our bond away."

I'd believed Alex's words and thought he did, too.

Talking about our crazy first time beside the ocean diverted us from my subpoena, and we moved into the bedroom. Afterward, Alex headed back out to salt the walk.

Valentine's Day, Alex brought a rose. "Bet Ramona never gave you one of these," he said.

"If she had, it wouldn't have come in this plastic test tube."

A few mornings later, Alex pinched his moussed hair into points. He rinsed his hands in my bubble bath and said, "You were lovers, right?"

"You could be talking about anybody."

He soaped me.

"Don't worry," he said. "I know I was your first. But don't you wish you'd been one of her sex slaves? You could have learned her techniques and tried them out on me."

"That's right. You know how much I like that stuff."

"Maybe you'd like it more."

"I doubt that."

He sat on the side of the tub. "Why didn't you tell me, Pauline? It hurts me that you didn't."

"It's a sob story. And there's not much to tell."

I didn't want to talk about Ramona again before the trial, especially not to him. My testimony would have the odd cast of a public truth he could react to along with everyone else. If I told him now, the story would enter our relationship. It would live in this house with us. It already lived in my office. I could breathe in there, alone with it, but I couldn't take it out of the room, let alone share it. I liked how Alex saw me and feared any change that might take him away. Holding onto him was worth any flak he gave me.

"We should tell each other everything. Like lovers do."

"Why, so we can hurt each other?"

"So we can know each other and stay open."

"What we call the truth comes back on us."

"Where is that coming from? What does it even mean? We don't do that." He dipped a face cloth in the water then wrung it over me. I took it and spread it out on my chest.

"We would, eventually. Like these sex slave comments. You suspect that since Ramona and James allegedly had sex slaves, that I might have been one of them."

"I was making a joke. About sex. About something I'd like to try that I thought you might, too."

"That's sensitive of you."

"How is that insensitive? You were friends, you said. What else aren't you telling me?"

"We were friends. Since I'm part of a trial about this issue, since I did know the woman accused of these things, you might not try to get me to do them."

"I'm not trying to get you to do the things she's accused of doing but to have some fun with me. Remember that?"

I sucked in a long, audible breath then heaved it out. He stood. "I don't know what you're about. You don't want me to feel sorry for you. But you're making it hard for me to feel anything." He walked out, leaving the door open and the air cool. I drained the water and stayed in the tub. He came back in, coat on, and held out a towel. My skin squeaked against the porcelain as I stood up and let him wrap me.

"Kiss me, so I can go to work," he said. I gripped his sleeves and kissed hard, relieved. He never went out without saying goodbye.

Fighting with Alex left me revved up, contrite, driven. After breakfast, I put on Nirvana, closed my eyes, and flung my body around. By the end of the song, I screamed along: "A de-nial. A de-nial."

Panting, I took my library book into my office. I'd given up reading slave narratives from the southern U.S. and returned to true crimes. I'd found one about a girl in California whose captor kept her for seven years, two of which she spent in a box under his waterbed. Through a vent hole she could see a patch of driveway beneath his mobile home. Each day she was let out for a couple of hours to empty her bedpan, eat leftovers, read the Bible. Her hair fell out, her muscles atrophied, and her vision dimmed. She signed a contract and wore a gold collar she believed would identify her to other men who would seize her if she escaped. She had a slave name, K.

I identified with K, though it didn't make sense. My dad

lived half an hour away and Jenna wrote letters. Until recently, I'd had a job, and besides, Alex and I didn't have that kind of relationship. He joked about tying me up — for fun, he'd said. He didn't torture me or keep me in a box, and he wouldn't. I hated that I wanted to read about K. I hated what Alex must see in me when I brought up serial killers and he changed the subject. That I liked to read about other people's pain, that it didn't hurt me. It did, though. What K suffered shocked me, and I cried sometimes, though more often she showed up in my dreams. When I read about her watching dawn rise through her vent hole, I got the idea for a pinhole camera.

A hole in the box's door could project an inverted and reversed image on the opposite wall. I could record what I saw on a piece of photographic paper. It wouldn't make sense in the novel, but I wanted to try it anyway. Besides, I hadn't worked on that novel since the interview with the cops.

Canvas covered the chicken wire on the box. The cone measured six feet long and three feet high at its wide end. Like K, I couldn't stand up.

Today, I sat inside. The walls needed lining so the chicken wire wouldn't print hexagons on my skin. I hung a quilt over the opening then climbed in again. I'd seal the box with opaque tape and spray-paint the lining flat black. A pinhole camera had to be light-tight.

"Polly" came on, a song about a man torturing a girl. I'd read that the real girl, the one the song was based on, had escaped her captor. The line "she's just as bored as me" made the rage sound sympathetic and hollow. I could relate.

I nudged the honeycombed foam with my palms, soles, knees, and back. I rolled my face against the wire, pursed my lips and tongued the chromic thread, the spongy give. In here, the panic wound down a notch. I'd touched this calm in a sex shop once when I'd let Jenna belt me into a straitjacket as a gag. When I had the door and lining in place, I could crawl in here and sink into the familiar numbness.

The weekend before the trial started, we went to a wedding at a hippie church in the Ottawa Valley. I was marvelling at the bride's grey hempen braids when the pastor said, "Through submitting to Adam, Eve is submitting to God."

The bearded pastor clasped his hands in front of his rainbow-banded robe. Jeans and earth shoes peeked out from beneath the hem.

"While Eve submits to Adam," he said, "and by submit we mean that she hands him her will and asks him to bend it to God's ways, she must cultivate her own will that it may be tested through Adam, and that where it is true, she have it shown right back to her and know it to be so. Now I won't say they submit to each other — Adam, as the man, is next to God — but only that Eve must not give up her *self*, or her soul. As Adam's wife, she is part of a holy union made robust because she ministers her own will for the purpose of its submission to Adam, and through Adam, to God."

I studied the women. The unadorned faces with warty cheeks and unplucked chins. The grey-pink skin and shapeless hair. And the strong, sinless eyes. As if they held no secrets. Or if they did, they defied anyone to wrong them for doing so.

My hand crept over to Alex's, and he pressed it. For courage or sustenance, I couldn't tell. Maybe forgiveness. I hoped so.

Earlier in the week, Alex had brought a print of a Japanese silk painting home from a History of Surgery exhibit at the College of Medicine. He'd unrolled it on our living room floor and secured it with art books.

In the foreground, a woman lies serenely in a flowing turquoise and white kimono, head on a red and white bolster, hair tied off her face with a maroon scarf and spilling over her pillow, eyes shut. A man kneels beside her on a bolster, hands on thighs. To his left sits a black lacquer box with an open drawer and a red lacquer teapot with platter and spoon. To his right, a grey-haired geisha in glasses fans the prone woman.

"It dates from the end of the eighteenth century," Alex said. "That's Seishu Hanoka using a preparation of datura."

"Datura. Didn't Carlos Castaneda?"

"No, not him. That voodoo zombie guy."

"*The Serpent and the Rainbow*," we said in unison. I touched my ring.

Alex continued: "Hanoka used his datura preparation as an anaesthetic agent given by mouth. This print shows Hanoka experimenting on his wife. See that spoon? The teapot? That's how he administered the preparation."

The wife is talcum white while the husband and his helper are a healthy olive. The wife lies stark-faced, at rest, arms straight at her sides. Hanoka looks placid, yet keen.

I leaned over the print. A ceremonial knife sits above the tied waist of Hanoka's pants, its handle obscured by the pattern of the silk.

A slip of paper in the bag said Seishu Hanoka founded the Hanoka School of Surgery in Japan. Even if he'd orchestrated his wife's surrender, I suspected her sacrifice held pleasure, and intent. After the anaesthesia discovery, such a wife, her will well-tended, would insist her body be subject to further experiment. For her husband's career, of course, but for her own reasons besides.

The couple stood to take their vows. With Alex, I had submitted by agreeing not to make the relationship official and by showing only a loveable version of myself. I'd handed over nothing in bed, though. I stayed shy there, left his kinky offerings unsampled. Since our fight in the bathroom, I'd thought about my testimony at Ramona's trial and whether Alex would react more to the fact of my secret or to what it revealed.

I returned his hand-squeeze. A woman strummed guitar and a man played the organ as we all stood and sang "Here Comes the Sun." Alex and I spent the rest of the ceremony Morse code–pressing each other's palms, eyes on a life-sized felt hanging of God banishing Adam and Eve from the Garden of Eden.

When the Ramona Hawkes trial started on March 30, 1992, I added the morning news to my routine. Anchor Tad Stiles read highlights of the opening remarks while the screen showed text superimposed on shots of Ramona's arrest.

The Crown Attorney for Peel County, Ron Laurie, planned to make full use of James Hawkes's vices. Certain statements rattled me. "Nobody forced Ramona Hawkes to drug and sexually assault anybody." "Ramona Hawkes was no paralyzed victim." "She got caught up in a spiralling escalation of paraphilia that ended with her murdering her husband." I shrank at the term "sexually assault." Its invasiveness and its stigma. I didn't see how I'd ever get used to it.

Laurie's instructions to the jury struck hardest: "Look past the gender of the accused and examine the evidence. Ask yourself, who was in control? Who had the power? Ramona Hawkes wanted to commit crimes with her husband. When she found out he had fallen for someone else, she grew jealous and killed him. This woman before you did not murder out of a subjugated wife's fear for her life. Rather she acted from a calculating killer's need to eliminate a threat."

I scoured the papers but couldn't find the name of the woman who'd come between Ramona and James. It occurred to me that James, not the other woman, had provoked Ramona's jealousy, that Ramona did have feelings for her friends. We'd mattered.

Well, one of us had.

By day ten I was tuning in to the morning news as soon as Alex's tires squelched out of the driveway.

Tad Stiles came on: "Record lows in Alberta. Two home invasions at separate ends of Toronto overnight — and new details about Molly Sumner, today's sensational witness at the Ramona Hawkes trial. Next on *Good Morning Today!*"

After the commercials, a shot of Ramona, slate-eyed with a

white-blond fringe. I forgot to blink. *GMT!* liked this photo of her posing in a merry widow for her husband, the victim.

Then Tad Stiles: "The trial of Ramona Hawkes continues today with the first of her teenage friends appearing before Justice Walter Larraby. The Crown lobbied unsuccessfully for her to use a pseudonym. Though she was under eighteen when she knew the Hawkeses, nobody sexually assaulted Molly Sumner."

Flash on the merry widow, then on *GMT!*'s favourite. Ramona stands by an unlit campfire, one foot on a log, one fist balled into her hip. The other hand, raised, grips the feet of a jackrabbit carcass. Its ears flop like hair.

"Strange to imagine someone so beautiful as evil," Tad Stiles blurted.

Beautifulevil. Once again, they hadn't shown the scar photo. Last week, after the defence introduced it into evidence during his cross-examination of Identification Officer Leif Peterson, the *Toronto Telstar* ran it and *American Murderer* showed it as part of a ten-minute spot, but I hadn't seen it since. Probably because the photograph of Ramona's scars was not alluring, nor even sad. It was cold, and it was grim. It promoted extremes. In it, Ramona lifts a hospital gown to expose a jagged welt across each thigh. She's tucked her hair under a cap and wears no makeup. Her dark eyes stare past the camera. She has no other visible marks. At the trial, it had come out that doctors found nothing else, no bites, scratches, or welts.

The defence must have thought people would feel sorry for Ramona. People did. Nobody wanted to imagine a man hurting a woman like that. Though some, like Cynthia Fist, a columnist in the *Telstar*, agreed with the Crown. Cynthia Fist allowed that James Hawkes had likely caused the wounds. Yet there were intersecting marks, she noted, the sort of tentative test cuts a person might make before harming herself. She brought up Munchausen Syndrome, where a person self-inflicts injuries or presents symptoms in a quest for attention. She referred to Diane Downs, who shot herself in the arm after shooting her children. When the Crown suggested Ramona could have inflicted the wounds herself, Cynthia Fist agreed.

Ramona could have used a riding crop, Fist proposed, or a rope to scar her thighs. I figured knife, if she'd done it, the same knife she'd used on James. Why not? She probably got the idea right after she killed him. If she killed him. Cynthia Fist said the wounds looked fresher than Ramona claimed. Nobody had an answer. She could have done it, but that didn't mean she had.

I skipped breakfast and headed for the Lucky Dollar. It was too soon for reports of Molly Sumner's testimony, but the papers would tease out more details.

I saved Cynthia Fist's column for last. Whenever the trial bored her, she shifted focus to the periphery. A seasoned trial watcher, she believed the friends and relatives of the accused could erupt at any time in court.

"Darling little sociopath" has parents, too
By Cynthia Fist
Toronto Telstar

Toronto – The parents of accused murderess and sex offender Ramona Hawkes are a constant presence at her trial.

During a murder trial, the media will often assign blame to the parents for psychologically damaging their darling little sociopath. Good, honest people like Ivan and Petra Ksolva get lambasted for the slightest difference in their child-rearing practices.

Balderdash! What happened to personal responsibility? Ivan and Petra are as much victims of the crimes of their spawn as the parents of James Hawkes and the parents of any of the young women being exhibited at the trial. In fact, we should commend Ivan and Petra. They have fully (if misguidedly, in this reporter's opinion) supported their daughter

throughout her arrest and pre-trial incarceration.
And now here they are at the trial.
What parents! Above and beyond most.

Not everyone liked Cynthia Fist, but they read her. I did, too, because she said what she thought. I took courage from her.

I placed the folded paper on the fridge. The past few Christmases Alex and I had spent at his family cottage on Georgian Bay. I hadn't called my dad since convocation. He didn't match up well to Ramona's steadfast parents.

Reporters had revealed one new fact about Molly Sumner. She was fourteen when she first met Ramona Hawkes, who was fifteen. She was twenty-eight now, four years older than I was. Ramona wouldn't consider either of us for friendship today.

On *Heidi Roth-Lopez*, a panel discussed murderers. Dr. Sheldon Highman, a British specialist in North American crime, claimed murderers didn't "get caught." Rather they "self-revealed."

"Murderers decide on a subconscious level when they are ready to be found," said Dr. Highman.

Two men who'd served on juries at high-profile murder trials and a woman engaged to a serial killer on death row in Florida had said their pieces. Highman had the floor.

"Their crimes saturate them to the point where their secret leaks out," he said, "noticeable at first only to those who are looking. Some leave clues, a signature, so to speak, maybe an item abandoned at the scene of the crime, or a totem stolen. Often they engage in a relationship with the society out of which they have cast themselves, taunting it. They want their evil discovered so they can assume their rightful position as pariah, outcast, whipping post."

Heidi offered a moue to the audience then asked, "How does this theory apply to any of our current murderers?"

The audience pumped their arms in the air. Heidi squinted at Dr. Highman, his words a parade of barbed, distracting flowers. The other guests sat mute, hands in their laps.

"There is Ramona Hawkes," he said. The reason I was watching. "Ramona is a prime example," said Highman. "An outcast who could no longer contain her secret and thus signalled her desire to come into society, if only to assume her role as fallen woman. Killing her husband was the signal, not in and of itself, although the spouse in such a case is always the first suspect."

"You're saying she wanted to get caught? So she killed her husband?" Heidi's voice lilted up an octave at the end of each sentence.

"The defence would have us believe she was an abused wife," said Highman. "Though you'll notice no mention of this history was made until after she was charged with murder. A more distinct possibility is that the salacious rumours are true. Ramona and James did lure girls into sexual slavery, or some semblance thereof. As the Crown has suggested, one likely got too close to her husband for comfort and our Ramona took matters into her own hands."

Dr. Highman's lips and forehead glistened.

"For Ramona to kill James signalled that she'd had enough of this," he said.

"And how would you describe *this*?"

Highman scanned the audience as if he faced a horizon. "Ramona Hawkes is a classic case," he said. "She would have murdered eventually. Her obsessive behaviour had veered out of control, and she had to be stopped. Since no one else had any inkling of what the dear girl was up to, she stopped herself."

"By killing her husband?"

"Yes. Now you've got it."

Each day now, I got inside the box. Sometimes I lay with my head near the brass door and watched the phantom window the pinhole projected on the box's far wall. Sometimes I woke up hot from dreams of riding in a car with Ramona and K, nobody at the wheel. I ransacked the images, from James's bloodsprawl on his marital bed to Ramona cuffed, head bowed, stepping from the court wagon into the underground garage on the first day of her trial. It was important to see Ramona as no different from Myra Banks or Evelyn Dick. Violent. A murderess. Ramona in seamed stockings and a British accent. Ramona with a valise. If Ramona could kill James, could she have killed me? Sometimes I wished she had.

Ron Laurie had twenty-nine women ready to testify at the Ramona Hawkes trial. When Ramona's lawyer, Bill Witherson, challenged this use of similar fact evidence, Laurie countered that the patterns of her friendships constituted a "unique *modus operandi*" upon which her motive hinged. Justice Larraby ruled that six of the women could testify. Laurie moved successfully to have the names of the most recent two protected. Both were under eighteen, and one was alleging sexual assault, though the charge was part of a second indictment the Crown would try later. I was one of the six chosen as witnesses, but I was not under eighteen. They wouldn't protect my name.

Cynthia Fist wrote the same things about each witness.

Predator's "pattern" started young
By Cynthia Fist
Toronto Telstar

Toronto – A lovely young woman who narrowly escaped devastating consequences by virtue of age and

the "luck" of meeting Ramona Hawkes in her forma-
tive years, Molly Sumner is as much a victim as any
other, tainted by her association with this creature
who fed off her innocence and used her to grow into
the fearsome preying monster we witness each day
in Courtroom 7-2 ...

I wondered what she'd say about me.

Justice Larraby gave the Hawkes jury time off until the
Tuesday after Easter. The talk shows reverted to transvestite
love triangles and female gang warfare. I didn't buy the paper.

Alex emptied his gym bag into the basement washer. He
took off his T-shirt and tossed it on top. Aside from an oblong
beige stain on his left shoulder, he had unmarked skin that
flushed often, his muscles etched like dunes. He folded me into
a bear hug and I inhaled his cinnamon bite, fingers nestling in
the valley of his spine. Growling, he guided me into a kiss, my
hair in his fist.

I ferreted his scrubs out from the clothes pile. "Shouldn't
the hospital wash these for you?"

"Usually they do. I forgot to take them off before I went to the
gym. Don't worry. I didn't do much today. They're clean-ish."

I researched bloodstains in a book called *Handy's Household
Hints*. Wearing rubber gloves, I soaked then rinsed the scrubs in
a paste of cold water and meat tenderizing crystals from the
Lucky Dollar. Then I met Alex in bed.

He sidled onto me and pinned my arms to my sides. "Nobody
lets me do anything," he said.

"Who?"

"The hospital. I could perform surgery as well as anyone,
including Dr. Augustin. How else am I supposed to learn if I
can't practise my skill?" He'd complained this way before.
When we'd met in Foundations of Art at university, he'd griped
about an oil painting the prof assigned. He worked best with

watercolours, he'd said, and refused to use oils. He got a 0 and switched to pre-med.

"Show me your skill." I wriggled away and spread my arms. I met his eyes then closed mine and held my breath.

He lay on his side and leered. "That's what you say. But you never let me do anything either." He twirled the hem of my nightie with a finger. I moved closer and kissed him.

"Surgery. Dr. Hanoka practised on his wife." I kept my tone jokey, light. I wanted to go to a new place with him, but I didn't know how to get it started.

"The poster boy? He administered anaesthetic. He didn't cut her."

"So you say. Show me, then, on my body. How would you take out my appendix?" I lifted my nightie, what I usually waited for him to do.

"You'd have to take off that chastity belt for starters," he whispered near my ear. The edge had left his voice.

I turned off the lamp and slid out of my panties.

"Lights are helpful, too."

"If you're so good, you should be able to perform surgery in the dark." My belly shuddered then rose to meet his cold hand.

"First you're prepped," he said. "Shaved, washed. An orderly rolls you into the operating theatre on a gurney then transfers you to the table, supine. Then you're intubated and given general anaesthesia. Your abdomen is draped. There are blazing lights above and nurses to assist. I'd have my tools on a tray beside me. With my Metzenbaum scissors — I know you love the terminology —"

"Baby."

"I'd cut here, called McBurney's Point, and hold the incision open with a retractor. Then I'd reach in, snip the appendix free, clamp, suture."

He marked the line with his fingernail. My thighs stirred. "I wouldn't feel a thing."

"Not until you woke up."

"You'd have your fingers inside me."

"This is different. This is beneath the skin."

We were watching *The Ten Commandments* and eating Easter eggs when I announced I was going out of town for a while, up north, back to Haliburton maybe, to work on my novel. "I'll have to miss the trial," I said.

"Unless they un-subpoenaed you, I wouldn't advise it. You could get charged. They call it contempt of court."

"That cop, Detective Stanton, he phoned again. He took me to meet Ron Laurie, the Crown attorney. I had to go over my story, practise being cross-examined." My voice shrilled. The cops had given me a copy of the police statement with my answers to their questions about Ramona, but I wanted Alex to hear what I said on the stand, rather than read it at home. I grabbed his shoulder. "They won't protect my name, Alex, because I was eighteen. Oh, and I'm not supposed to go in the courtroom before I testify so I don't get influenced. They could charge me if I do. Most of it's in the news, though. All the girls are saying the same thing — that they acted out fairy tales and movies. Nothing sexual. What's the point of having me up too?"

"Maybe they think you'll say something different."

"I don't want to say anything."

"The question is, do you have anything to say?"

"The question is, why should a person have to talk if she doesn't want to?"

"A person shouldn't have to say anything at all," he said. Then he kissed me, what he did when he didn't want to fight. I snapped my face away. I wanted opposition, the okay to fling out all subjects, hurl fury at him.

"You're jittery. Anybody would be, no matter what kind of testimony they were giving. This is a murder trial. It may be inconsequential to you, but what you say could affect this woman's life and many others. That's enough to rattle anybody."

I let myself agree with him and reminded myself that the

Crown would ask about what my statement contained, nothing more. It calmed me that Alex wasn't prying, yet I half-wondered if he didn't care. What little control I had I felt slipping away as the date of my testimony grew closer.

"Come to bed," Alex said. He stood and took my arm. His voice, his mouth, stayed even. I teetered and a near-sob choked out. I rolled it into a laugh and let him pull me along.

"But the Red Sea," I said. "It hasn't been parted yet."

"Don't make me make that joke."

Later, half-kidding, I said, "I feel a cold coming on."

"Maybe you need a doctor."

"I need surgery. A long recovery. Something to make it hard to talk or think."

"Brain surgery. Or throat."

"What about the face? You could disguise me."

I rubbed his hips with my thighs while he hovered above and made fingernail dents on my temples and neck where he would cut.

"Not your face," he said. I closed my eyes as he moved the crotch of my panties aside. "I need to know it's still you."

"Why is Friday the holiday and not Monday?" Alex bit into his morning plum. "Anybody can die. Rebirth is the niftier trick."

"Don't complain. Maybe you'll see some stigmata today."

"One can only hope."

Inside the box, with the door closed, I pictured myself on the witness stand. Ramona might look right through me or give a sign — a wink, maybe, or a lip-curl. I didn't know which I'd prefer. I'd never told Alex and I'd never told my dad and I shouldn't have to tell anybody now. I didn't care if my testimony helped put Ramona in jail for murdering James. I didn't care about the future sex slaves I might keep from harm. I'd even stopped caring about K. If I could only forget everything so not telling was not lying. Who would know? Only Ramona, and she had no reason to spill. Though she might think I wanted to protect her. Ramona wouldn't understand shame.

St. Mary's Hospital was up the street from the courthouse. Alex had convinced me to drive in with him on Wednesday. But what would I do until then?

The answer came to me. Too bad if Ron wanted me out of the courtroom. I would see Ramona Hawkes.

Thirty-nine people stood in line outside the courthouse across from the obelisk and the sculpture of three soldiers on University Avenue. The sky was lightening over squared roofs, and headlights dimmed. At the end a grey-haired couple had set up woven Maple Leafs lawn chairs. Beside them, a girl sat cross-legged on the interlocking brick tying washers and bolts onto a black leather cord and singing, "An-ger is an energy." The Manson family came to mind, cross-legged outside Charlie's trial with Xs carved in their foreheads. Charlie had Xed himself first. With what? Maybe his fingernails. His long, dirty fingernails. The Manson girls heated bobby pins to red hot to burn their Xs then ripped the Xs open with needles.

After Alex left for work, I'd pinned up my hair and put on three sweatshirts, scrub pants, and Doc Martens and tucked my old fake ID into my pocket. At the last minute, I punched on a fedora, Alex's, from his artist days. I walked up to the highway and caught the bus into Toronto. I disliked driving in the city.

The crowd shuffled and a lawn chair bumped my knee. My heel landed on the girl's corduroy bell-bottom.

"Sorry," I said and stepped away. She licked her lips. Under a fatigue jacket and a down vest, her black T-shirt read "Too Drunk to Fuck." She looked familiar but like no one in particular. She stretched the collar and scratched at a tattoo on her breast.

"You get used to it."

"You've been here before?"

"Every day. Lots of us do. It's a drug."

How many days had I spent combing the newspapers when I could have disguised myself and come here, to the source?

"I'm waiting to see if they'll put her on the stand," the girl said. "Not likely. I'm Joy. This is my first." She tied the ends of the cord in a double knot then snipped them. She put the necklace over her head and dropped the washers under her shirt.

"Pauline. Mine, too."

"Why don't you sit? I'll make you one. The metal feels good on your skin. Like a piercing, without the pain."

More than ten people stood behind us now. "That's okay." I pictured the cold washers between Joy's breasts. I moved back and looked up. Buildings bar-graphed the sky.

"Everyone's buying her story," Joy said, standing. She had half a head on me. "Like Wanda Kake in the Beaconsfield Slaughter. They even had blood evidence, but Wanda looked good and spoke sweet and the jury let her off."

I remembered the blood on Alex's scrubs, the flutter I'd had later that night when we'd played surgery. I hadn't met someone who liked talking about murder in a while.

"That's because nobody wants to convict a woman," I said.

"They'll be making a big mistake if they let her go."

"Why do you think?"

"I don't know." Joy started another necklace. She told me she'd run away last year. She was catching up on what she'd missed at an alternative high school called FreeTeach. "My Canadian History project's on women who murder," she said. "This is my research."

I liked Joy. I hadn't connected with anyone this fast in years. Joy knew as much about this case as I did. I told her that I read murder stories and that I wrote them, but I didn't tell her I'd waited here once, outside Osgoode Hall, the summer after Grade 13. I didn't tell her about Ramona.

Security guards moved in, arms outstretched, and blocked the cordoned-off line. Television crews hauled equipment and barked into walkie-talkies. As the old couple folded up their lawn chairs, the lineup wobbled. Sunlight wrapped the buildings and drivers extinguished their lights. Joy fingered the necklace under her shirt, her hair swinging near her hips. She kept her eyes on mine until the court van splashed past and everything shifted. Then she smiled and I looked away.

Inside the courthouse, Joy headed for the stairwell.

"It's faster this way," she said. "We'll get better seats."

"You go ahead," I said. "I don't care where I sit, and I need the ladies'."

I passed the Crown Attorney's office. Maybe Ron was in there. He'd told me to wait in the hall outside the courtroom until my name was called when I came to testify. I moved into the crowd by the elevator.

Detective Stanton stood at the door as people filed into the courtroom. I hadn't expected him. I hesitated. He could charge me if he caught me at the trial before my testimony.

Someone pushed me, and I caught up to the old couple, who stood behind Joy now. When Stanton stopped her, she showed off her T-shirt, hands on hips. He didn't see me edge past. I found myself a seat by the far wall. Moments later, Joy plunked down beside me.

"That cop's a perv," she whispered.

A man in black biking tights sat down, and Joy slid closer.

"Sorry," she said, her leg resting against mine. She smelled like gasoline, maybe motor oil. I wanted to sniff her palms, her cuffs, chase down her scent.

As an escort officer led Ramona to her seat, I shivered, nauseous. To keep myself from jumping up and screaming, I sat on my hands and inspected on Ramona's clothes. The navy dress was boat-necked, the matching jacket too broad for her shoulders. The ends of a limp navy bow grazed each ear. The *Telstar*'s shot of Ramona descending from the court van had shown spice-toned hose and patent-leather pumps.

The overall effect was matronly, save for her face, which

she'd caked with foundation, crimson lipstick, and brown shadow blended up to the brow.

"Bitch," said Joy.

"You think so?"

A Plexiglas barrier enclosed Ramona's table. She faced the judge. Her blonde hair strobed between the spectators' heads. My cheeks prickled with sadness and a faint disgust. Ramona's body looked solid, heavy, like she might have trouble carrying it, more like my own now. I imagined a bulge of waist, a bloom of thigh. The raspy voice. The bulky cotton prison underwear. I grew hot and shucked my trench coat, conscious of how much fabric I was wearing.

I shifted away from Joy, who'd taken out a sketch pad and was roughing in the courtroom with a black felt tip. I rummaged in my bag for a pen.

It helped to think of what happened as someone else's story. Writing about Peck gave me access, let me put what happened outside myself. No matter how I shaped it, dressed it up, or hid it, the truth caught the light like water. Peck was me, and yet she wasn't. Nothing comforted me more. I found my pen and notebook and wrote.

Peck was wearing a Kashag Malamutes T-shirt over white cord shorts and leaning against the counter of Venus Video watching Bonnie and Clyde rob a bank the day the woman from the parking lot strode in wearing pink leopard print pedal-pushers and a ripped powder blue sweatshirt. Her platinum hair fanned up and out like plumage. Her glistening lips had a candy smell. Peck remembered the lip gloss. She remembered it bugging her.

chapter 4

The woman dropped a video on the counter. Peck fetched the case. *Black Emmanuelle*. The woman waited, black-rimmed eyes on the screen above the video game display.

"You could make your cheekbones look like hers," she said. "You've got her look."

Peck checked out Bonnie but couldn't get the resemblance. Bonnie was a delicate blonde, Peck square and dark. They both had small noses, but the woman hadn't mentioned small noses.

"What they're doing is romantic," the woman said. "Don't you think?"

Peck nodded. She found the name Mona Ksolva beside *Black Emmanuelle* on the rental card.

"Is your middle name Lisa?"

Mona smiled, teeth oily from the gloss. "Did you just move here?" she asked.

"A few weeks ago."

"You're the first person who's ever said that to me." Peck believed her.

Every third night, Mona rented a video. She rented *Smokey and the Bandit, The Getaway, Snow White,* and *Deep Throat.* The day she returned *The Collector,* she came back a couple of hours later and caught Peck watching Freddie and Miranda struggling in the rain.

"Good. She likes crime *and* horror."

"I was curious when you brought it back."

"Do you watch everything I watch?" Mona smoothed the ruffles on her tube top.

Peck drew in her lips. She had, even the pornos.

Mona laughed. "We should hang out. Why don't you come over tomorrow night? I'm on Covered Wagon Trail, Number 17."

"I get off at eight."

"We can have a girls' night."

"Okay," Peck said. She'd never had a girls' night.

Mona's house was three streets away, on the side of Westwoods that bordered on fields. Hank said people who paid more for houses near nature would get ripped off when developers tore up these fields to build more houses in a few years.

Covered Wagon Trail was a cul-de-sac featuring a wagon wheel planted with striped petunias in the middle of a curb-lined grass circle. The houses here had more personal touches than the ones on Hartley Horse Way. Black shutters, morning glory trellises, and lion head door knockers distinguished one house from the next. The residents here could show more pride. These houses were detached.

Mona opened the door in a ribbed blue tank and the leopard print pants. She'd tied a rolled-up pink leopard bandana around her head.

Peck tripped on a pair of hockey skates inside the front door.

"My fiancé's. He's not here."

Mona offered her wine from a box with a spout. "I'll walk you home," she said. "Wine doesn't smell up your breath."

"My dad wouldn't care."

She stuck to pop, and so did Mona. They took microwave popcorn and brownies into the den and turned on music videos. The nubbly beige couch was long enough for Mona to stretch out her legs without hitting Peck, who faced front.

Winnie the Pooh came on. Mona did the voices. Peck laughed until she hiccupped.

Mona walked her home even though she hadn't had wine. "Wouldn't want you to get lost," Mona said, winking.

Mona moved around a lot. She twitched and touched to make a point and had toppled giggling with her head in Peck's lap. She'd kept it there until the end of *Winnie the Pooh*.

Walking, Mona kept close. When their bare arms brushed, she didn't move away. Neither did Peck. They stayed like that until Hartley Horse.

At home, Hank dozed in front of the Jays game. Peck sank on her bed. Nothing much had happened. She and Mona hadn't said anything interesting, and she hadn't told Mona much about herself. But she felt inspired. Like a change. Light spilled through her at the drift of Mona's hair on her thigh. She stayed awake until the birds started, fainter than at home in Kashag but there. Lulled, Peck rolled herself into sleep.

Peck went to Toronto for the first time that July, 1985. It was a Wednesday, her day off from Venus Video. She wore white shorts with a red and white striped tee, white plastic sunglasses, pink jelly sandals, and a red and gold purse — all bought with the summer clothes money from Hank. She was saving her pay for downtown.

On her way to Mona's, she practised the sexy crossover walk Mona had taught her. The plastic grids dug at her feet.

Mona waited on the driveway in a strapless black denim dress with a brass diagonal zipper from skirt to top, a studded collar, and black wedge espadrilles that laced her calves like

Roman sandals. Her platinum hair slicked up and out. She said she'd called in sick to Henderson, Albert & Tizz.

At Kennedy Road they caught a bus to the Four Corners of Brampton, where Queen met Main and each corner had a bank. Mona insisted they stop at Kirby's Bakery for homemade doughnuts dipped in sugar. The doughnuts tasted good. From then on, Peck would get a doughnut from Kirby's whenever she passed the Four Corners.

At the station, they bought return tickets and sat on a bench outside. The green and white bus wheezed in front of them, door locked.

A burn stung Peck's thighs. She removed a jelly. Red grooves latticed her foot. Mona's lip curled, and Peck inched the sandal back on. Mona stroked gloss on her lips then dipped the wand and offered it to her. She had grown to like the candy smell. She liked the slick feel of the fuzzy tip. The way her lips rolled together. She wanted her own lip gloss, but Mona said she'd have to get invited to a makeup party.

The Looking Glass Head Shop dwelled below street level in a recessed concrete area. Two speakers mounted over the door broadcasted David Bowie singing, "We've got five years, my brain hurts a lot." Peck plucked the back seam of her shorts and followed Mona inside.

The thick air smelled of light sweat and strawberry incense. She sneezed.

"Everything okay?" Mona smiled beneath her Ray-Bans.

She nodded. The store smelled like her mom.

Pictures of musicians and black satin banners covered every inch of wall. Racks stuffed with Indian cotton shirts and skirts, concert T-shirts, and leatherwear crowded the floor space. The glass counter displayed pipes, rings, earrings, bracelets, chains, belt buckles, lighters, headbands, and feather clips.

Mona headed for the chained-up leather clothes to find a

bustier. Peck drifted over to the poster carousel. She flipped the frames, stopping at one of John, Paul, George, and Ringo in their Sergeant Pepper moustaches and satin uniforms.

Peck's mom had clipped feathers in her Cher hair and gone braless under Indian cotton smocks. She'd smoked spiced hand-rolleds on the porch and liked to watch the merry, relaxed hippies kaleidoscoped in the sixties documentaries. Nobody could expect her to stay up north in Kashag Township with her ordinary husband and daughter. She had escaped into the muted golden blur where she belonged.

Though her mom had one part wrong. Peck wasn't ordinary. If she wanted to, she could run away to north Scotland where only a man as talented as Paul McCartney could meet and fall in love with her.

Peck bought strawberry incense, an Indian cotton blouse, and a black satin banner of Lennon in leather against a brick wall in Hamburg. Rock and roll.

After lunch, Mona treated her to a movie that played year-round in the Eaton Centre basement. They took seats near the front. There were no previews, only red lips singing against a black screen. The camera zoomed in on a church wedding, and the audience shouted "Slut!" at Janet, the female lead, and "Asshole!" at her boyfriend, Brad. Three people sang along and danced at the front. No one complained that they blocked the screen.

When Janet soloed, Mona whispered, "Isn't her voice pretty?" A chorus of "Slut!" drowned out Peck's answer.

When Brad and Janet, stranded in the rain, entered the Frankenstein Place, the audience rushed forward. Mona dragged her up by the hand. Colours washed faces. The Time Warp dance looked easy, though the instructions got lost in the whoops. At the end, everyone fell into the aisle. Peck hesitated, but Mona yanked her to the sticky floor as the music wound down. Soon, the audience scrambled up. Peck, too. With what came next, sitting down was not an option.

Spangled platform heels tapped a rhythm in a descending

cage elevator. The camera panned up a silver-collared satin cape to glossy black-red lips against white skin and swooping midnight blue eye shadow under bemused brows. When the creature threw off his cape, Peck forgot her body. She had to know more. Fat pearls laced the thick neck. Flesh bulged from the sparkly vest, taut panties, and fishnets. The intimate voice rolled over sax squawks and guitar thrusts, melting hard. Peck wanted him. She wanted to be him, too. In the course of one song, one image, this man, Frank N. Furter, supplanted her Paul McCartney sheep farm nanny fantasies. Welcome to Transylvania. Having a wonderful time, Mum. Wish you were here.

chapter 5

I looked up. Joy sketched a tall brunette who stretched her cardigan sleeves over her fists as the bailiff swore her in. I returned to my story and ended up missing the start of Lyndsey Franklin's testimony. That was fine. One look at her paisley A-line skirt and floral scarf convinced me she was not a woman I liked.

Mid-morning I stopped and chewed my pen. Joy stopped, too, and our eyes met. Lyndsey Franklin was dabbing her cheeks with a tissue. Joy leaned over and whispered, "She won't look at her."

"Who?"

"Lyndsey Franklin. She won't look at Ramona. See?"

Joy was right. When Lyndsey Franklin wasn't watching the Crown, she stared at the judge. Or at her lap. Never at Ramona. Who could blame her? The back of Ramona's head gave me shivers enough.

Lyndsey Franklin tucked the tissue into her sweater cuff

and said, "Imagine what might have happened if my family hadn't moved away from Cloud Lake when we did."

I held in a scream. My friendship with Ramona wouldn't have happened, that's what. I stood. *What is it?* Joy mouthed, and I nudged her knee. She shifted, and I launched myself down the row, past the court officer, and into the hall. In the ladies' room, I lurched into a stall and locked the door.

Testifying meant facing Ramona. I'd been bracing myself to tell the court — and Alex — what had happened. It sank in now that I'd be telling Ramona, too.

Someone had wedged a folded yellow paper behind the toilet paper dispenser. I unfolded it and read an ad for the Buttercup International Hostel. I memorized the address on Dundas and stowed the flyer in my bag. Such signs didn't come often enough. Could I do what it asked, follow the map and walk to the hostel? I'd have to pay with cash from the bank machine and sleep in my clothes. Alex, I'd worry about later, let him think I skipped out on the trial. He'd remember me saying I was going up north. Or I could call and lie, tell him I had a sunrise meeting with the detectives, easier to stay in town. More true, I could say I needed space. He'd understand. I did need space, even one step away from love, its snugness and its revelation. His finger-traced incision a promise I hoped (and feared) he'd keep. Worrying about Alex, about escaping from this trial and maybe my life, calmed me down about Ramona. I stayed in the hall outside the courtroom until after lunch, but I decided nothing.

At the end of the day, I lingered in Courtroom 7-2, waiting for Joy to leave. Hours of listening to another woman tell stories of her teenage friendship with Ramona had wrung me out. Joy sat sideways on the cushioned bench and hugged a knee to her chest.

"Great ring," she said. She tapped the snake heads. "When'd you get married?"

"We're not, officially." I leaned on the seat in front of me.

"You live together?"

"We call each other husband and wife and wear these. I feel married. We're going to spend our lives together." Whatever this girl asked, I answered. I had missed having a female friend. Jenna kept extending her teaching contract and had no plans to come back to Canada. I wanted time alone, but my urge to talk took over and I plunged ahead: "Marriage is too conventional. The actual wedding. The ritual. We will have one, someday. It's a formality."

"Why say husband and wife, then, and wear rings? Why pretend?"

"We're not. We did our own ceremony and we're bonded. We just haven't had a wedding and done the legal thing."

"Who gives a fuck if other people don't get what you do and the way you do it?"

"I don't." I stood.

"Are you writing something about the trial? Because you don't look like a reporter."

"I am a writer. But don't worry. You won't have heard of me. Listen, I should go or I'll miss my bus. It was good to meet you." I meant what I said and ended up holding her hand for a minute before easing past her to the aisle. I hurried across the hall and ran down the escalator.

It never mattered that others understand about me and Alex. When we came back in love from our East Coast trip, nobody said a word about the rings or the name change, but I didn't care. Alex and I were a fact. No outside opinion could alter us. I would marry him if he asked. I needed him to stay, though, and marriage was no guarantee of that.

Our first Saturday night in Flats Mills, Alex had driven me to a pub in a town called Neville Roscoe. We were sharing chicken fingers when he said, "I kissed Sharon Jenkins."

By the time I swallowed, he'd finished the story. Sharon, a skinny poet with coiled black hair and droopy eyelids, had kissed him in the kitchen at an end-of-term party. He'd kissed back. It surprised him that nobody had told me. Some friends I had.

"I didn't know a thing," I said.

"We're through. I told her."

"You needed to tell her you were through after one kiss?"

"She expected more."

"Of course she did."

"I wanted her to know I was with you." He drew out his words as if he were having a breakthrough feeling.

"Everyone knows you're with me. We had that party at our apartment, remember? Why did she need reminding?"

"Don't you see?" He lowered his lids.

I did see. He thought he'd done a good turn. Perhaps he had. But I could see nothing beyond a kiss on the lips of saggy-eyed Sharon Jenkins and the knowledge that during that moment, he had left me. We didn't talk about it again and had paved over the silence with a ritual of walking and smoking up that I'd believed signalled a new closeness between us but that I saw now was as dead in its way as what I'd felt after my mother left and with Ramona. I'd started making the box that week.

I walked past the courthouse pillars onto Armoury Street. Raindrops made rings and bubbles on the plashy sidewalk. Thunder snarled below the traffic din. Hair unpinned and hatless in the rain, I walked up University. Away from the cocoon of my house and routines, I dwelled on each imagined moment between Sharon and Alex. On the edge of an outraged wallow, I reached Dundas, where I considered turning left and wandering over to the Buttercup Hostel. Instead, I headed toward Bay.

Too late, I reached the terminal. The last express bus had gone and the next one left in two hours and took longer. Alex would soon finish his shift, if he wasn't working overtime. I could wait for a drive with him, but I wanted to get home first so he wouldn't know I'd come here today.

I bought a *Telstar* and found a bench. I was halfway through Cynthia Fist's column about the second trial of a man previously acquitted of killing a nine-year-old girl when a hand grabbed my paper and shook it.

"I saw you come in here," Joy said. Her hair hung heavy with water.

"What are you, following me?" I was glad to see her.

"I passed you in my car and thought maybe you'd want a ride. You could hitch, but I never do, not after that girl on the 401."

"I only hitched once," I said. "I don't advise it."

"Let me drive you. I'm free tonight."

"Why would you want to? You don't even know where I live. The bus will come along eventually. They always do."

"I don't know why. I like you, Pauline. We could hang out, be trial buddies."

"I won't be watching the trial again."

"Suit yourself," Joy said. "But I'm here now."

I rubbed the flyer's fold. I could ditch the bus, tell Joy I had friends to stay with or get her to drop me at the hostel — and not leave Alex. The Buttercup Hostel provided linen and promised coin lockers, free coffee and doughnuts, and no frills. I could stay one night. I could wake up in a dorm bed, ride a streetcar to the courthouse and testify, and not leave Alex.

"A ride with me will save you money," Joy said. "I won't even charge for gas."

"You obviously don't know how far away I live."

"Sure I do. You told me. Also, you could give me your opinion of the trial. It'll help my project." Joy fingered her belt buckle. I suspected a new piercing.

"Which project?" Lyndsey Franklin's testimony crowded my mind. I couldn't remember much of what Joy had told me.

"The one about Ramona Hawkes. For my school." Joy swung her right leg forward and back. Her hem caught a candy wrapper. Alex would see a night away from home as a statement against him no matter how I pitched it. I needed space but not explanations, and I wanted someone to talk with more than I wanted anything else.

I folded the newspaper and said, "Where are you parked?"

In the car, Joy rolled her hair and let it fall into her lap. I hitched my seat forward.

"Did you know Ramona?" Joy asked as she pulled out.

"What makes you say that?"

"How you reacted when she came into the courtroom. You acted jittery."

"I'm glad she didn't see me." I didn't like Joy figuring me out.

"Is that why you're dressed like that?"

"How do you know I don't dress like this every day?" My layers bulged out around the seat belt. I donned Alex's hat and tilted it.

"You came into the courthouse all bundled up and glancing about, and when I found you at the bus station, you'd changed. You're more yourself."

"You don't even know me. How can you tell?"

"I just can."

"I'm testifying tomorrow. That's what I'm doing."

"You were her friend." She glanced at me under lowered eyelids.

"Did you guess that too?"

When she didn't answer, I softened my tone. "Earlier?"

"Maybe, but I didn't see how you could have been."

"Why not? You don't think Ramona would have been my friend?" *Too abrupt. She means nothing by it.* Her every word nipped my skin. I felt small and miserable and judged. I wanted to strike back. I opted for the truth.

"I didn't think witnesses could attend the trial," Joy said. "When they're not testifying."

"They can't — we can't. We're not supposed to, anyway, or we could get charged. I was incognito today. You're right, though. I grew up in Cloud Lake. I was friends with Ramona."

Joy swung the car under a railway bridge and headed north on Black Creek Drive. Disarmed or nonchalant — I couldn't tell — Joy shifted subjects.

"Lyndsey Franklin had intensity," she said. "She knew about James."

"Not much."

"She knew he was in law school. She knew he met Ramona at a cocktail party and how much in love they were."

"That's all in the paper," I said. "She didn't have any inside track to James. None of them did. The others at least had the decency not to pretend to more of a friendship than they had." Lyndsey Franklin's testimony had vexed me. Though talking about it felt good. I missed Alex.

"Lyndsey Franklin wanted to prove she was more connected to Ramona." Joy pointed the car into the centre lane of the freeway. The car ahead flashed brake lights but didn't slow.

"Maybe, but she wasn't."

"Ramona gave her wine," Joy said. "And they slept in the same bed one night when James was away. She said they only hugged, though. Yeah, right."

"It doesn't mean a thing. It's a competition to her. She has to be superior and she's not. After the others you'll forget her. Why else would Ron Laurie call all of Ramona's friends chronologically? He wants to show where she started out and where she ended up."

"He wants to show that she's a sex offender, Pauline." There was that term, as hard to hear as "sexual assault." Joy continued: "He wants to show she's got a 'unique *modus operandi.*' That's what he said. It's a quote."

"True, but Lyndsey Franklin wasn't special or long-lasting. And yet she knows she was different from the friends Ramona had before her. She is right. With James in her life full-time, Ramona was ready to go to a new level."

"Is that what you did?" Subtle Joy had managed to steer our talk around to her fixation. I didn't mind.

I could have lied, or said, "Wait and see." Ramona and I did have a rare intensity. I'd known it since I met her, even though I didn't find out she had other friends until this trial. Maybe James was the catalyst. How unfair that Ramona had two such powerful relationships at the same time. But she did. When James increased her volume, she found someone to distort it.

That someone was me. Not enough years had passed for her to find another friend like me.

I faced Joy. My neck throbbed.

"It was different." I couldn't give Ramona up, not here. "But I never saw her again after."

"After what?"

"After we were no longer friends."

"How about the murder?"

"James?"

Joy nodded.

I cracked my window and raised my nose to the air. "I don't know what to say about that."

When we reached the turnoff for Flats Mills, Joy announced she had to pee. "I'll be quick," she said. "Promise."

My heartbeat zipped. Highway 89 was darker than the freeway. After a while the air looked blue and the far-off buildings shades of black. An oncoming car lit up Joy's face, hair pulled to the side, the stem of her neck. She held herself like a bird, her centre of movement somewhere deep between her hips, chin down. She wore glasses to drive. I squinted and the light washed away.

"Sure," I made myself say, "but you can't stay. My husband's coming home."

Our lights were off. Alex wasn't back. Joy shot out of the car and huddled on the stoop, her hands in her pockets. Water dribbled from the awning.

Inside, I hung my coat on a peg. Joy toed off her sneakers and followed me to the living room. None of my friends had seen this house. Jenna had left for Czechoslovakia before we moved here. The others had scattered after university. I felt nervous showing Joy the house. Defeated, too, yet happy. The red walls sat stalwart behind the clutter of nudes. I didn't know where to look.

Joy did not have the same problem. She stepped neatly over the Hanoka poster and headed for a Mapplethorpe print of a male torso arcing back against a half-white, half-black backdrop. "I didn't know you were into art," Joy said. She moved pigeon-toed from nude to nude, her hands in L-frames at shoulder level. She arched her torso, inhaling each picture. Her bottom lip protruded, wet, red, plump. "Are any of these yours?"

"I used to dabble but now I write. Anyway, I'd never hang one of my pieces here."

"Where do you write, other than in courtrooms?"

"In my study, in the second bedroom."

"Can I see? I love seeing where people make things." Joy bounced on the balls of her tube-socked feet. Her hair had dried away from her face in a haze. She drummed her fingers on her collarbone and bit her lip. I could stand behind her, hands on her hips, and guide her around the room in a dance. I could take her arm, steer her into the bedroom. She could see my actions as friendly. She might go along with them. Either way my desire would hover between us. I saw the beauty of Ramona's approach. She'd taken me sideways, made me think I wanted her before she made any moves. What would Ramona do here, with Joy? Ramona had had a program, a grand plan for me. With Joy there was heat and fear. Anything that happened I wanted to come from her.

"There's nothing to see. And you don't have time." I remembered the box. I could show her, find out what she thought it meant.

"My parents won't care if I'm late. They'll be glad I'm home. They should be proud I'm having this, that we're talking about art and writing."

"We aren't really." She'd recognized our connection, too.

Joy squinted and pointed to the Hanoka print. "This one on the floor. It's strange. Ordinary."

I squatted and traced my finger along Hanoka's kimono. When I reached the knife, my hand twitched.

"I suppose it's both," I said.

"It doesn't fit with the others."

"No. Nobody's nude."

"So you'll let me?"

"See my room? Of course. A quick glance, though," I said. "And no questions."

Joy stroked the cone's little door.

"Can I go in?"

"That's what it's for."

She scuttled to the back and hugged her knees.

"It's like a fort. Can you close it?" She poked her head out and said, "Am I asking too many questions?"

"No. Not that. I can shut you in, sure. Go back where you were. But only for one minute, that's all, then you should leave."

Joy sat back, legs folded, her position different from mine. There was room for two.

I held the handle for the entire minute. When I opened it up, Joy hadn't moved. I squatted, poked my head in.

"It would be hard to breathe after a while."

"Possibly."

"Can't you tell me what it's for?"

"I said no questions. Besides, you'd laugh. It's not like I'm a sculptor."

"Does it have anything to do with —"

"Ramona? My husband?"

"I didn't mean —"

"I know. Anyway, it is its own thing now."

"I won't laugh if you tell me."

"Fine. In the novel I was writing, I had a character, a sculptor, who made a box like this. Instead of writing, I spent my time making this box. I wanted to know how a sculptor thought first-hand. But I was avoiding the book."

"Why was she making the box?"

"She was studying slaves in the southern U.S. and had read

about the tiny spaces used to hide runaway slaves. She made the box and conjured up a ghost."

"A slave ghost."

"Mortifying, isn't it? Yes. I wrote a long outline, but making the box was the most interesting part. Now I sit in it."

"It's a good place to think, probably."

"It is. The book was pretentious and improbable. And, I guess, derivative. It wasn't what I wanted to write." For the first time in a while, I thought about K. Since reading about her, I'd forgotten the runaway slaves who'd inspired my character's box.

"You know what you want to write now."

"I do."

"You've been in here?" I had both hands inside. She pushed at the sides as if to make the walls expand.

"Yes, but only alone. I've never tried two."

"There's room." She shifted, flopped her knees to the side.

"Are you sure?" I got in and turned, my back on her arm, my feet on the door lip. I nudged her thigh to make space and ended up falling against her.

"Pull in your feet. Let's close the door. See what that's like." She held my elbow. I reached across her and we were in darkness. She shifted my shoulders until my head lay beside hers, her hair whiskery on my ear, my legs raised, feet hanging. My hand against her thigh. I eased the pressure, then rubbed. Her hand covered mine.

"Pauline —"

I levered myself around and brought my face close to hers. I sent breath to every point our bodies touched but took care to hold myself away.

"Pauline, I can't breathe and your knee is in my stomach." Her foot bashed the door open. I backed away. I hit my head and rolled out, ungainly. I scrambled up.

Joy slid forward on her bum and hopped out. She circled the cone pigeon-toed, hands raised in a frame. She smoothed her palms over the black canvas then pressed her cheek against it.

"I love it. And I won't tell anybody."

"Thank you." I shook, sweat-chilled, uncertain. Everything she said could mean something else. In the room's light I lost my nerve.

I had failed Joy, and the box. I felt the same way I did when someone read one of my stories, no matter how much praise I got. Showing made it not mine somehow, not in the same way, and the loss smarted.

With Joy in the bathroom, I closed up the room. I hadn't planned on anybody ever seeing the box. Alex, sure, because I lived with him, but he took little interest in my work these days. I perked up when I remembered that Joy had missed the hole I'd pierced in the brass door. She didn't know the box was a pinhole camera.

Joy crouched in the foyer like a toddler. She made big loops in her laces before winding them around, under, and through each other. Her hair veiled her knees. When she stood, she flung it back and met my eyes.

"It felt good in there," she said. "Like I could stay inside for a long time."

My chest seized. I opened the door on the leaking night.

"You could."

After Joy left, I had enough time to change out of my bulky clothes and watch a game show before Alex came home. Once he got his coat off, I handed him a whisky and poured myself one. He joined me on the couch.

"Where are your scrubs?"

"Thought I'd spare you. Witnesses at murder trials shouldn't be doing laundry the night before they testify. It's a rule."

I buried my face in his shirt, happy to see him, relieved.

"Something's different," he said, scanning the room. He sniffed my hair.

"I didn't move anything." I checked the floor for stains, but Joy had taken her shoes off. Had she dripped on the poster? I couldn't tell from the couch.

"It's you. You smell like rain. Were you out walking today?"

"I was. Lots." I sank against a cushion.

"Must be nice to have the time."

"It is nice, Alex. It is." My unemployment insurance would run out soon. Alex said he would support me, but he meant in the future, once he had a practice established, not now, while he was an intern. We didn't speak about me getting a job, though Alex made the odd dig. I gave straight answers every time.

In bed, he said, "They made me do preps today. Like a nurse. It's unreal. I could've worn my scrubs to dinner, they were that clean."

"Let's try it again," I said. "You and me. I'm ready." After seeing Ramona, I wanted to wipe away what I'd have to say on the stand tomorrow. Alex would know soon enough. Tonight I needed to focus on anything but her.

"Me too. What?"

"What we played at last night."

He got up and ran a bath then gathered some tools and changed into his scrubs. In the bath, I drank two neat whiskys then lay on a towel, eyes closed, as he foamed then shaved me with a razor dipped in a bowl of warm water. He stroked the blade over each spot twice, then blotted me dry.

"Are you operating there, doctor?"

"I'll be completing all the necessary procedures. Now, hush, or I'll have to call Nurse Meany."

He talked me through another appendectomy as he traced mock incisions above my skin with a scalpel. I itched with effort. A shift might mean a cut. Earlier, he'd grazed his own finger to show me the easy flag of blood. He used clothespins, sewing needles, and makeup sponges to replace the tools he didn't have. A warm chain snaked my thighs. At the end, he flourished a length of thread.

"There's no scar," I said.

"See how good I am." He straddled me, muscled me down.

"That's some bedside manner you have, doctor."

I woke up on my side. The blind angled open. A bulb of moonlight shone through the gap. I found Alex's hand. He hung on to my wrist, awake now, too. My mind burned and hissed. A stabbing rage entered my arms. I wanted violence. I wanted it from him.

"I'm prepped. What about my disguise?"

"What?"

"My face." I flexed my wrist. He tensed, then he let go.

"We were playing." His voice croaked.

"I know, but we haven't played that." I switched on the light and pulled down the blind. He grimaced. He wore a scrub shirt and nothing else. I handed him his knife and he raised himself on one elbow. His eyes flickered with hurt and something like compassion and a hard eagerness that made him look away. I inched closer on my back.

"Not your face, Pauline. I said. Not even as a game."

"Here. My hair can cover it." It scared me to bully him this way. I never had before, not in bed. I counted on him saying yes, even to things he didn't want to do, in case I wouldn't try anything new again.

I shifted onto my side so my belly met his, and fixed my hair behind my ear. He stretched his neck and folded his arm, fingers delicate on the tool. I gripped his wrist, pulled his hand close. I felt a jolt, wetness, then pain. All sound wedged in my throat. Liquid trickled along my cheek. He scrambled up and blotted me with sponges. They soaked pink then red, then a dull brown.

Heartbeats hurdled around my chest. I wanted to strike him and I wanted him to go further, wherever that went. This moment felt more real than the rings, the husband-wife labels, the bond, anything. The old deadness came, what I'd called love before I'd spent time inside Alex's love for me. What Ramona had pulled from me. What my mother had. Why was I feeling it now, with Alex, after five years?

Ramona.

"Take this," he said. He pressed my hand and the towel against my temple and left the room. An apology formed itself around my chest, and a hope that I hadn't angered him. He came back with the white plastic first aid box. He took the towel from my hand and dropped it on the floor.

"Stay still," he said when I stroked his arm. I shoved my hands under the covers and gulped back my wanting. He swabbed alcohol and taped a gauze pad in place. His palms pleated. No needle. No flourish of thread. Trembling but adept, he wouldn't meet my eyes.

He dropped cotton balls on the floor then climbed into bed and shut out the light. We lay close without holding each other. Then he was easing away, his body contained and impersonal. He covered me and left the room and ran water. I rubbed myself through my nightgown then reached under to curl my palm around the fine bareness. I fell asleep to pipes banging.

I woke up early, swathed to my ears in the duvet, warm. Sunbeams lazed on the blind slats. He slept with his arms over his head, a whistle in his breath.

"Alex."

He didn't answer. I pulled his plaid flannel robe over my nightie. Red dots speckled the blue sheets. In the mirror, I latched onto my gritty eyes. The brown irises and bushy lashes. The veined violet lids. I gripped the dresser as I peeled off the clotted gauze. A brown thread etched my hairline, a cat's scratch. Ragged fingernails. Or a dull blade.

He had done it. We had, for I'd made him, and I'd watched, thrill-eyed. We'd reached the limits of his love and expanded mine. I dug at my temple, against the pain. My face a sick, happy crumple. My nails smeared red.

Alex liked a plum before work. A woman at the Bev's Donuts on Black Creek Drive had an apple fritter and a double

double ready for him each weekday at 7:00 a.m. Last night, late, I'd poured boiling water over curls of ramen noodles in two orange bowls. I had shaken in powder from two foil squares and covered the bowls with plates. I cooked and Alex did the dishes. I walked into the kitchen now, afloat in tears. Two plates, two bowls, and two forks sat in the green rubber tray.

Back in the bedroom, I stood over the futon. Sunlight striped the duvet. Alex hadn't moved, but he would. I wanted to wake him. I didn't want him to touch me. Twenty minutes until the alarm rang. I didn't want to leave. I wanted never to see this bedroom again. I dropped my nightie on the towel. My skin was clammy, my armpits rank. I put on one of yesterday's sweatshirts over jeans. I went out the front door without locking it. I was leaving. I wanted him to find me.

I parked the Hustler at the gas station across from the Buttercup Hostel. Runnels of steam wove along the wet asphalt in the sun. The sky to the north and toward the lake was a darkening lavender-grey that threatened snow.

Dundas Street had empty sidewalks but constant traffic. The only people stood at the self-serve tanks, gas hoses lolling from gloveless hands, beige trench coats on some, pastel parkas on others.

I stood at the curb. I faced the sun and waited for the street to be free of cars.

When the traffic kept flowing, I stepped out and peered up the hill.

After a long time, a man driving a Jeep pulled out to make a left then stopped, waving me across.

Thank you, I mouthed.

He honked and mouthed, *Go.*

I crossed.

The Buttercup Hostel was a yellow three-storey house wedged between a building with a sign advertising Killex Pest

Control and a storefront that said Hoi Cao Nien Viet Nam Elderly, where a web of fading vines and a cluster of ceramic Buddhas, herons, gazelles, pigs, ducks, horses, and cows crowded a fly-specked window.

The porch creaked. I stood between a yellow wrought iron bench and a pop machine, and knocked. A streetcar lumbered past, and I knocked again. A man in blue velour track pants let me into a lobby plastered with hand-lettered signs.

"You want a room?" he asked. "I'm the proprietor. John Soules."

I registered as Peck Brown and paid sixty dollars for three nights. Ron Laurie had said my testimony might take three days. "Stay over if it makes it easier," he'd said. In less than two hours I would be on the stand. Alex would be awake now. He might think he dreamed last night. He'd see I'd left. He'd expect me home later. Better to stay away until I'd told my story in court.

"We can't enter the women's dorm until after ten," John Soules said. "To protect their privacy. But I can give you a tour of the rest."

"I'll come back tonight."

I had appointments all day, I told him. Business. I didn't mention the trial.

John Soules wrote me a receipt while I scarfed my free coffee and two honey-dips. He gave me the dorm room key. His shift ended at ten, but he came back on at four.

"I'll see you later," I said. I wiped doughnut glaze on my jeans.

"Will do."

Ten minutes before the trial started, Ron Laurie came out of the elevator, robes on, carrying a coffee and pulling his foot-wide black case on a dolly. I sat near a group of women in a row of plastic chairs bolted to the wall outside the wooden doors of

Courtroom 7-2. As Ron approached, the women wandered off. I took off Alex's fedora and finger-combed my bangs. The cut smarted when I touched it, but I could otherwise forget it was there.

Ron Laurie was a short, peach-toned man with a white pelt of hair. He was talking before he reached me. Catchphrases. "I'm under obligation to provide." "What I'm planning to say." "You should talk a lot about." He instructed me to wait in the hall with Detective Stanton and left to find his assistant. Stanton stood near the door. He nodded when Ron said his name and raised an eyebrow at me.

In our interview, Ron had told me what questions to expect. Today, I had other thoughts on my mind. Alex had cut me. I had left without a kiss or a goodbye. Alex believed in love's rituals. Though I'd scoffed, each change did ripple, throw the whole of love into question. I'd rented a bed. I should have written a note. Easier to leave than explain. Now I was acting like my mother, and like Ramona. I'd keep my answers on the stand brief.

When my name came over the pager, the commissionaire, a short woman in a tie and a navy blazer with an Ontario crest, came out to get me. She led me past a table that held several file boxes to the witness box. I sat and faced the court, the jury to my left, Ron Laurie and the defence, Bill Witherson, and their teams in front, Justice Larraby above to my right. A box of tissues rested on the ledge.

I stated my name as Pauline Elizabeth Brown and spelled it. My mouth tasted like pennies, and I swallowed after almost every word of my oath. Near the end, I glanced at Ramona on the glassed-in prisoner's dock. The courtroom artist, Desiree White, hadn't got her right. Desiree White had complained to a reporter the week before that she found Ramona Hawkes's face impossible to capture, too changeable. Anger thickened my voice. "Nothing but the drooth," I said, "so help me Mod."

Ramona faced front, glassy-eyed. I tried to focus on Ron's questions and not stare at her poker face. I struggled to stay still under the scrutiny of so many: courtroom artists, Joy, trial groupies, reporters, jury, lawyers, the judge, and Ramona herself. The effort made it hard to find words to tell my story. Thankfully, though, words did come.

A woman typed what I said into a machine. After the trial I could buy the transcripts, anybody could. Though I had no character to hide behind, I told it like I was writing it down. I told Peck's story and I let myself believe it wasn't mine.

Excerpt from Transcript
RAMONA HAWKES
v
HER MAJESTY THE QUEEN:

_____

April 22, 1992
Toronto, Ontario

_____

MR. LAURIE:	Ms. Brown, what did you know about the accused? About her hobbies, shall we say.
MS. BROWN:	We liked to do all the same things. Only we talked about them more than we did them.
MR. LAURIE:	How did you find out you both liked the same activities?
MS. BROWN:	She asked and when I told her what I liked, she told me she liked it, too.
MR. LAURIE:	What did the accused do that was different from you?
MS. BROWN:	She loved her fiancé. I didn't have a boyfriend.

chapter 6

In the month since Peck first saw Mona Ksolva at Venus Video, she hadn't met Jim Hawkes. She went over to 17 Covered Wagon Trail most evenings, but Jim worked late at his summer job at Hench & Smeaton on Bay Street in Toronto. Sometimes, he stayed overnight and showered at the office. Pictures of Mona crowded the fridge and dotted the mantle, but the house displayed no images of Jim.

Peck and Mona were lounging under a hot, white sky on attached cedar Muskoka chairs when Mona told her she'd had sex with Jim in the men's room half an hour after they'd met. On the slatted table between them, a tabloid lay open to a spread about Ted Bundy's devotion to Buddhism.

At the law school Christmas pub, Mona told her, Jim was wearing a false cast on his arm Bundy-style, asking women for help. The women knew him and ignored him.

When he dropped his briefcase in front of Mona and stuttered while gathering the papers together with one hand, she laughed. She found him charming and perverse in a way none of those budding corporate, tax, and real estate lawyers understood.

He braced his hips on the sweating cinder-block wall and lifted her onto him. They locked eyes and she didn't utter a sound. The brick scraped her knees.

"I went home with him," Mona said, "and never left." She rubbed baby oil on one foot with the toes of the other. "Next summer we're making it official. August 10. Jim will be taking the bar ads then. Can you get my back?"

Mona untied the neck strings of her orange and lime bikini. As she leaned forward, the triangles drooped and she said, "Did I tell you he's going into criminal? Everyone's interested in murderers."

Peck squirted a puddle of oil and moved her fingers over Mona's back. It was bonier than her own, and very brown.

"Not many lawyers choose criminal," Mona said. "Ethically, some struggle with the idea of client confidentiality. A lot of people who go into law, believe it or not, have a high moral stance and find it hard to imagine representing someone evil."

"Do lawyers even know if their clients are guilty?" In the true crimes Peck had read, many lawyers did know their clients were guilty, but they didn't care. Others put up a wall to block out any details that didn't serve their clients.

"A lot don't want to so they can build their case better. But Jim won't have a problem accepting his clients' guilt. He'll probably lap up the gory details, knowing him."

When Mona had first showed her the den at 17 Covered Wagon Trail, Peck had nodded at the built-in teak bookshelves lined with true crimes.

"Every one ever written, according to Jim," Mona had said.

Peck kept quiet about her own interest in murderers. She didn't talk to Hank about it either. Though she hadn't read a true crime or written a murder story starring her mother since she'd moved. Maybe she'd changed.

Mona angled a full-length shot of Bundy toward Peck and

said, "He's not so great. Not cute enough to fool me with a broken arm or lame foot."

Peck studied the photo as if she'd never seen Bundy before. Already she might do whatever Mona suggested. Keeping her fascination with murder a secret gave her a feeling of power.

"He's old but not cute. I wouldn't notice him on the street."

"That's the quality that worked for him. Pleasant innocuousness. You have a thing about age, don't you?" Mona flicked Peck's oiled arm.

"I don't look at someone like him" — Peck pointed at Bundy in his mid-twenties — "and think about whether he's cute or not. He's closer to my dad's age than mine."

"That bugs you?"

"Sure. He's a man."

Mona laughed.

"A full-grown man! And I hardly even have boobs yet."

Mona cupped hers and said, "These aren't much bigger. Some men prefer little bitties."

Peck snorted.

"Your dad's not that old," Mona said. "I've seen him drive by a couple of times. He's only in his thirties."

"He turned forty on Father's Day."

"That's young. Mine's in his fifties."

"He's not young to me."

Peck fiddled with her strap hook. Mona reached over.

"Let me do your back. A tan will make you sexier."

"I'll get freckles."

Mona oiled her back and over her shoulders. "They're not that small," she said as she tucked a quick finger under Peck's left boob. Peck shuddered and stayed put.

"By the way," Mona said, "Jim is older than me. Seven years. He took time off to travel and work so he's older than most of the other law students. You won't like him."

"Why?"

"He's in the Ted Bundy age range. But you should meet him so you can see for yourself. How he's got murder in him. He'd never do it, but it's there."

Peck gulped half of the syrupy rum and Tab she'd been avoiding all afternoon. Mona arranged her bikini top over herself.

Peck's eyes watered. She had murder in her too, her mother's gift, but she couldn't show Mona yet. She needed to hold something back.

"I identify with Rapunzel," Mona was saying. "I had an original mother, a gypsy mother, who gave me this name, a name the mother who raised me wanted to take away. She didn't want to call me Mona. She called me *Ramona* instead."

They were trekking to the mall along treeless sidewalks past identical brick houses and toy-littered lawns. The heat muscled their bodies like a dense, endless mattress. Mona often took the bus but said she liked to walk in the summer because she could get a better all-over tan. Peck had her Venus Video cheque tucked in the bum pocket of her baby blue shorts. She was planning to get a manicure kit.

Mona knew she lived alone with Hank. Whenever Mona asked about her mother, she said, "I'd rather not talk about her," and Mona dropped it.

"She is a powerful, evil witch, my mother," Mona continued. "Both mothers are. She would only let me escape that house with a man, though it means nothing to her unless I'm married. Which will happen soon enough."

"How do you know about Jim, though?"

Mona reached behind Peck and adjusted her slipping tank straps.

"Know what about Jim?"

Mona wore a black tube top with tube sleeves and a white denim mini with a pink lace hem, her shoulders sugar brown.

"How do you know he's not evil, too? That he doesn't have a secret?"

"Why would someone evil save me from someone evil? That's not how it works. Besides, Jim's not like that. I'm smart and I love him and I know. It's not that complicated. Jim climbed up my hair and rescued me from the no-personality tower my parents locked me in. Everything was perfect there, but I had no life. None at all, just my beauty wasting away."

"How you can trust that a guy is okay?"

"You do."

Mona linked her arm and steered her across Kennedy toward Middle Mall.

"Besides, I know Jim's secrets. And my secret is to be part of them."

At Super Drug, Mona proposed writing a play about Rapunzel.

"We'll buy a notebook," she said. "We can act it out as we go and you can write it up."

Peck inspected a vinyl lizard skin manicure kit. She hadn't mentioned writing her murder stories to Mona. "We're kind of old for that."

Mona rubbed Peck's wrist and said, "It'll be different when we do it, *because* we're older. Do you know Anne Sexton? She wrote about Rapunzel. 'A rose must have a stem.' It's rude, but true. We can take her poem and interpret it as a play. We did this in English all the time."

"In what, Grade 8?"

"In night school. It's the best way to understand the story, especially if you're creative like we are."

Mona thought of her as creative.

"We're not little kids playing pretend," Mona said. "We're women creating a work of art. Even if it is a kids' story. We have to start somewhere."

They bought three notebooks, one for characters, one for dialogue, and one for setting. That evening they performed the scene where the witch takes the baby Rapunzel away from her loving parents. Peck played the mother and Mona, the witch. Later, Peck would become the witch and Mona, the grown-up Rapunzel.

As the mother, Peck gave up the baby too readily, without enough emotion. They went over and over this scene.

"She doesn't want the witch to see what she's feeling," Peck said.

"She's a mother. It is natural for her to feel sadness and loss, and guilt, at giving up her daughter."

"Wouldn't she be angry at the witch for taking her?"

"She's saving her own life. She knows her daughter will be safe."

"How?"

"She's convinced by the witch's charm."

"But witches aren't charming."

"I didn't say that. I said her *charm*. A witch has magic at her disposal, including charms or spells, which, when cast, make the other person give the witch what she most wants. Watch."

Peck held the teddy bear baby again and again as Mona entered the room with the sexy swagger of a much fuller woman, a big-hipped outlaw whose mouth widened in hunger when she saw the bundle. The palms stroking the rolling hips, the fingers diving into the dusky cleavage, the rouged lips and coal eyes made Peck agree that this long-anticipated child of love, the only baby likely at this late stage, was worth giving away to such a spirited, warm creature. Warm? Hot, more like it! Her words sizzled and spat, fat on a fire, and Peck succumbed.

She didn't believe herself as the mother, though.

Mona consoled her. "The mother is not that important. Always remember that. The evil witch is. And Rapunzel, especially her. Now that you've seen the witch — you saw her, didn't you? I did. I hope you did. I was her. She was here and I was inside her. You can do that, too, and when you do, I'll be Rapunzel and we can find a tower room and everything can take place."

It had happened. Mona had changed into the witch, and Peck had become the mother. They'd made the story together. Not even Jim could share that.

At home, Peck started with the words they'd said, the easiest and least interesting part. Then she described the characters. Her pen ate up pages as she captured the witch's over-ripe body and rotting core. Finally her favourite part, the tower. She laboured long after Hank had come in, fixed a drink, showered, then closed his bedroom door. When she stopped, she had a series of sketches of the brick tower with no door and one tiny window that housed her beautiful captive. More and more, as she brought the prison to life, she identified with the witch's need to make this girl her own.

"You've missed her essence," Mona complained, though she loved the tower drawings. They sat on Mona's king-sized waterbed, bare legs wrapped in the black and gold quilted satin cover.

"She's perfect," Peck said. She reached for her notebook, but Mona wouldn't let it go. Peck continued. "Rapunzel is beautiful. The witch wants to hide her from the world so nobody else can appreciate her."

"True," said Mona, "but she doesn't know this baby will turn out beautiful when she cuts the deal. She could grow into an ugly troll for all the witch knows. In her greed, she takes that chance."

"If she doesn't want beauty, what does she want?"

"Youth. A girl she can possess so she can have constant access to what she covets." Mona handed her a sheet of paper where she'd typed "RAPUNZEL by Anne Sexton."

"Read the first three lines."

Peck read, "A woman / who loves a woman / is forever young." She pushed the paper away.

"It's not about *that*, is it?" Peck said, certain Mona was mocking her

"Keep it. I typed it out for you. Sure it is. She wants Rapunzel in every way, the way the mother wants the salad root. Everybody wants something. You just have to find out what it is."

"So she doesn't want to *be* young. She wants to have someone who is young? To be with her?" Both lamps shone but the room stayed dark with the curtains pulled.

"Maybe she isn't even that old," Mona said. "Did she seem that old to you?"

"Not *old*, not like an old lady or a grandmother."

"Too old to have a baby? I think she is young enough to have a baby but she can't find a man to give her one. Or she is cursed with this need for youth and she wants a live doll to recapture what she's lost."

"Maybe she wants life. Maybe the curse is that she is in a dead place." Peck shifted on her haunches. She understood the witch more than she'd thought. Mona met her eyes and swayed a wave between them.

"Maybe it's the same thing. She loves Rapunzel. Remember, this witch would consume this girl if that's what it took to meet her need. Instead she locks Rapunzel up and visits every day to fawn over the prize she has stolen from the rest of the world. That's what love feels like to her."

For the tower scenes, they shut the bedroom door in case Jim came home, and Peck became the rewritten witch tending to Mona as the grown captive. Playing a fairy-tale character in Mona's bedroom felt awkward, but when she looked at Mona, Peck knew the witch's greedy love for Rapunzel. As the witch, she could do what she wanted to Rapunzel and Mona would let her. She didn't dare wonder what Mona might allow outside of the roles.

They used no costumes or wigs. Peck wrote the words and they acted the story and then she was in it. Mona, too. She saw Rapunzel, the hair more tangled, woody, and dull than she'd expected, frayed, like a well-worn rope. The witch's heavier breasts and hips shaped themselves over Peck's torso. Her skin shadowed, and she swelled into the room ready to seduce and provoke. A filament lit this body, goading her each time to close in, clasp her captive back to front, rock her. Her body would stop at nothing to possess the creature she'd had the luck to grow for her very own.

Before she climbed down Rapunzel's hair, the witch dubbed one area of the tower off-limits. At first Peck squirmed at wielding such power, but as the sinful woman settled under her skin, she made her choices grandly. "Stay away from my letters," the witch declared. "Keep out of the bathroom." She banned Rapunzel from examining the books, the closet, even the refrigerator.

Midway through the play Peck changed roles. The prince shinnied up the braids into Rapunzel's cell. Unlike the witch, he kept his hands off Rapunzel, preferring to state his love instead. Together, he and Rapunzel duped the witch. Their favourite game became raiding her forbidden zone.

The illicit lovers pounced on the witch's desk and pored over her papers as a team. Their delight was mutual whenever they found a taboo item — a loose-leaf copy of *Regina v. Truscott*, say, or an unloaded .22 rifle. Maybe the fifth time they acted out Rapunzel, they discovered the stack of crime scene photographs in the sock drawer.

Though Mona later claimed she knew about the photos, Rapunzel's surprise and horror seemed genuine.

The photos were 8" x 10" and glossy. Some were black and white, but most were in lurid colour. The top photo showed a fat woman in a housedress and cardigan, lying face down in the middle of a kitchen floor. The skewed table held alcohol bottles, glasses, ashtrays, cigarette packages, bowls, and a double-bladed axe stained the same dark as most of the speckled linoleum. Most riveting was the pulpy, matted mess the axe had made of the back of the woman's head.

The prince and Rapunzel stood together, their breathing shallow. Their arms brushed as they flipped through photo after gory photo revealed during the frenzy of tossing black sock rolls from the drawer.

Peck forgot the game and herself in those suspended moments looking at badly lit depictions of domestic mayhem. Some bodies lay in living rooms, some in bedrooms. One sprawled in the driveway beside a station wagon. Many had died in kitchens. All crimes of passion. Wives more often, but a few well-stabbed and shot husbands in there, too.

"I told you he had murder in him."

She couldn't figure out whether Mona was playing the game or whether she'd gone back to her real self. Since Peck still saw Rapunzel, she said nothing and skipped out on cue.

The witch waited a long time in the hall, but when she sauntered into the bedroom, the smug, returning captor, nothing had moved. Mona sat amidst scattered sock bundles, the photos in her hands. Peck shook the witch off her skin. Mona drank in the images, not sharing. Her sudden retreat from their game got Peck talking.

"I've seen some of those already," Peck said. She reached for the pile, but Mona wouldn't let go.

"The fire skeleton," Peck continued. "I know that one. It happened in a rooming house, right downtown Toronto, near Yonge Street. And the woman in the frilly nightgown, stabbed on the knotted bedsheets? That one wasn't so long ago, and they haven't charged anyone. They're pretty sure it's the husband, but he had some stab wounds too and claimed he made a break and ran for the phone so he could save his kids."

Mona swivelled her head with the ease of a sun-full iguana.

"What ..." She paused for so long Peck opened her mouth. "... are you talking about?"

"Those photos," Peck said. "Jim's books, I know about all the murders in them. I've read them, and I know the details." She didn't mention the murder stories she'd written, or Malcolm Salter's crime album. She liked that Mona thought she didn't have any experience with guys.

"Same as Jim."

"The same."

"Why didn't you say anything?"

"I didn't want you to think I was pretending to know about murder, like Jim does, to impress you. I started by reading my mother's murder books, after she left."

Mona studied the photo stack.

Peck waited. Then, nervous, feeling like an intruder, she stood to leave.

"You impressed me anyway. And I'm sorry about your mother. That's the paradox of mothers. They give you life then kill you, slowly or otherwise."

Exposed, Peck helped Mona put away the photos and socks. Their relationship had shifted. Peck was not some new girl in the neighbourhood who liked to shop and had a flair for acting and art. Her obsession with murder connected her with the fiancé Mona adored. Peck had given up part of her story and lost her slight power. In return, she and Mona grew closer. Not a bad trade after all.

Apco Moulding closed down the last two weeks of August, so Hank had holidays. He wanted to take Peck back to Kashag. She refused.

"I have a job, Dad. Like you wanted. I'm not giving that up."

"You'll have to when school starts. Quit two weeks early and come north with me, catch up with old friends."

"I don't have any."

"Sure you do." Hank rhymed off a list of girls her age in Kashag whose parents he knew. "Oh, and the Sergeant's kid, Malcolm. Can't forget him."

She didn't care about going back to Kashag, not even to see Malcolm. The thought of kissing him made her tired. She couldn't reconnect with people she'd never connected with in the first place. Hank, they'd want to see. The whole county would throw its arms wide, hang banners, organize parades, and stage an arena dance to greet its beloved son. But not his coal lump of a daughter. Most folks probably only remembered he had a daughter because she was important to *him* and they wanted his esteem.

Peck had to return sometime, but not yet. They'd just moved. She had many reasons to hate Westwoods. But here she had her job, and she had Mona.

Besides, aspects of this lifeless place, where buildings repeated themselves in an effort to sell dreams of space and ownership, had captivated Peck. Westwoods's embrace of the average confirmed her misgivings about the sameness of people. Isolation made sense here. People in Westwoods didn't notice her. Neighbours here reacted to a new person with the same vacancy as they did to the line of matching two-storeys with front garages facing up and down this street and the next and the next and the next.

Peck got to keep the job if she agreed to go north on the long weekend. Her stance softened when she realized she'd become the girl Hank had fashioned in his mind's eye. She did have a friendship here.

She just wasn't ready to tell him about Mona.

Hank's vacation coincided with Jim Hawkes's time off.

When Peck called now, Mona answered with a fakey voice and cut her conversations short. Peck pictured Mona and Jim sharing the receiver, rolling eyes, laughing.

She hated every day she didn't see or talk to Mona. She crammed her feelings into a one-sided correspondence that rivalled her outpourings to Paul McCartney.

When not writing, she designed locations. She planned to make models of the tower prisons and castle abattoirs and present them to Mona. Even though together she and Mona saw the same slimy stone walls and barred windows, she needed fetishes to keep Jim and Hank from coming between them.

She wrote a new play called Hall of Mirrors about a princess who passes a cursed crone's test in a hall of mirrors and finds out her fiancé — a baron — is a murderer. After the sorcerer's spell lifts, the princess escapes with her new friend, now young and beautiful, to make a life together far away from the savage groom.

The first time Peck saw Jim Hawkes, he was sitting on the couch with his back to her, arm thrown around Mona's shoulder. Hank faced them in his recliner. Jim's neck sported a copper burn. Below his shaved hair a pale stripe lay like a vein of fat. Mona turned, then Jim. He flashed Peck a smile that crinkled his eyes.

"Look, honey, we've been invited to a party," Hank said.

She snatched the purple card from his hand, flustered at his enthusiasm and easy gratitude. Ever since she got her first birthday party invitation, the same one as everyone else in her class, she had taken care to erase such eagerness from her tone. Hank could afford delight. Hank got invitations all the time.

Seeing Mona in a belted gauze dress snuggling into Jim and winking at Hank unnerved her. She could appreciate Hank's appeal. Yet Mona had looked at her that way. She didn't like Mona sharing that private look around, especially with Hank.

The tiny card had puffy mauve flowers gathered by a ribbon heart. Inside, Peck found details of Jim and Mona's engagement party, Saturday at 2:00 p.m. at 17 Covered Wagon Trail. Mona hadn't mentioned the party before.

"I wanted you to meet Jim first," Mona said. "We came over to invite your father, too."

Peck located another source of discomfort about this scenario: Hank's glee at exposing the parts of her life she'd laboured to stow away for herself. He would think he could see inside her. She cringed at the prospect. She craved a place where she and Mona created the rules, wrote the lines, and built the tower together without anyone's interference.

Jim's gaze didn't waver. She wanted to stare back, but she had a hard time meeting people's eyes, especially new people in close quarters under parental scrutiny.

Mona glanced at Jim and back at Hank, then, without either man catching her, gave Peck a wink that said, *This is one of those things we have to do. We'll find a way to make this fun.*

She believed the wink. It was only a stupid party. She'd gone to lots of stupid parties with Hank. No big deal. It had nothing to do with her and Mona. She'd tell Mona about *Hall of Mirrors* tomorrow and they could act it out. Maybe they'd carry their world into the party.

"I need Peck's help," Mona said. "I'd like her to stay overnight a few days early, with your permission of course, Mr. Brown."

"Will you please stop calling me that?" Hank folded his arms over his Kashag Search and Rescue T-shirt.

"*Hank.* Jim is so busy I need all the help I can get."

"As long as it's not the long weekend, I'm happy to share her."

Jim stretched and walked to the gun rack. "These are something else," he said. "You use them?"

"Every year," Hank said. "Well, the one. The other needs fixing. Maybe I'll take it in this week."

"So you hunt. Don't meet many like you. No offence. Around here most people have lost touch with nature and our true place within the order of things."

Hank raised out of the recliner on the heels of his hands. "It's family tradition," he said, "but that's not why I do it."

"I understand. It's about the relationship between you and the animal."

"Sure. Some guys shoot anything that moves, but folks get hurt that way. There's a lot of waiting. It takes patience."

"Right." Jim glanced at Mona. "You follow the animal's track. You blend with the environment and fit into the fabric of the animal's life like a shadow."

"People say it's for sport, but that's not true with us."

"That's because the animal knows you are there and knows why. Your destiny and the quarry's are bound up in a power greater than you."

"Fair enough, though we're not spiritual like the Natives, thanking the Creator and all that. We do use every part of the animal, short of boiling the hooves down into a glue. I pickle the meat, tan the hide. Peck helps."

"Indeed," Jim said. He studied her the way he had the deer carcass photos. Peck shrank into her seat. She considered getting up to go to the bathroom.

"Do you hunt yourself, Jim?"

"Yes, Mr. Brown, I suppose you could say I do."

"*Hank.*"

"Hank."

Mona stood and said they had to go. Jim steered her out the door, hand on her tailbone. As they cut across the lawn, he turned and met Peck's eyes. Peck worked her arms under her shirt and held her sides while Mona and her fiancé got into the car and drove away.

Peck had planned to stay over at Mona's another night, before Rapunzel, before they spoke what Mona called soul-talk. Hank had had an overnight shift, so she hadn't told him.

On the waterbed, she and Mona leafed through copies of *Circus* and *Tiger Beat*. Mona talked about her friend Zilja, who had an apartment in Toronto and gave blow jobs for cash. Zilja modelled in mall fashion shows, too, but BJs paid. Zilja was saving for a house.

Mona brought out a red vinyl case of 45s. She sang the ones Peck chose, humming over the lyrics she didn't know.

Peck whisper-sang along with "Imagine." Mona acted as if she didn't hear. Thankful, Peck sang louder.

Sliding mirrored doors along one wall led to a walk-in closet with its own lights and built-in seats and mirror. Mona had saved all her clothes since before high school. She modelled her green and gold cheerleader's outfit with pompoms then her spandex pants with gold lamé heels.

"Your turn." Mona presented a zippered vinyl T-shirt, spangled tap shorts, and tights with horizontal black and white stripes.

"Your stuff won't fit me."

"Sure it will. We're the same height and a lot of it's stretchy. Zilja tries my things on all the time and she's half a foot taller."

The mention of Zilja got Peck on her feet. Unlike Mona, she couldn't change with someone else in the room. Maybe Mona could because she had a fiancé and friends who sold BJs, but as an only child who lived with her dad, Peck liked her privacy. Mona picked out a strapless black velvet gown with a rhinestone-clipped bow across the chest instead. Then Peck slipped into the closet and eased the lock into place.

Her bra straps looped down her arms, and her chest puffed out. She held her arms against the half-done-up zip.

"Try the next one braless," Mona said. "To get the full effect."

Peck chose Mona's prom dress, a turquoise taffeta. She liked the sleek lining and the straps carving into her shoulders. When Mona clapped and said, "Yes, that's it," she went back and squished into a leather mini, a sparkly blue batwing top, and spiked pumps, and strutted out. She wished she had makeup.

Mona had her clothes off. She rolled back, thighs together, knees against her forehead. Magazines, 45s, and clothes tumbled into the centre, and she swept them away before landing on her back then flipping onto her side.

"Nasty."

The nearest 45 had a butterfly on the label. Peck couldn't look at Mona's brown-all-over body for long.

Mona jumped up and brushed past Peck into the closet. Peck stood inert and pulsing. The shiny spread rippled. She quieted herself. Mona was acting normal. She wasn't. Mona changed in front of her, peed with the bathroom door open, grabbed her hand, played with her hair. Girlfriends acted that way with one another. She had never had a best girlfriend. She'd had Malcolm.

Mona came out in a black leather merry widow with leather panties and thigh-high boots.

"I've wanted to show you this one for a while. But I wasn't sure how you'd react, if you'd think I'm strange."

Peck kept her eyes on Mona's face.

"I could tell you'd be okay with it when you came out wearing that."

Peck's thighs felt clammy where they touched. She tugged at the leather mini.

Mona slid the closet door across and faced the full-length mirror. She ran her thumb along a jutted hip, bent and stroked her thighs. The bustier rested close and high on her chest, hiding any cleavage. She straightened and crossed one foot in front of the other, fluffing her hair with both hands.

"Try it."

Mona swung full circle, smile big.

"I don't think so, Mona."

"Come on. It'll look good. When else will you have the chance? You never would in a store. Do it now when it's safe."

Hands on her hips, Mona swivelled and rolled her shoulders.

"Why don't you come up to the lab, and see what's on the slab," she drawled like Frank Furter.

As Mona threw each piece out of the closet, Peck placed it on her lap. Mona emerged nude. She knelt beside Peck, held the front of the corset against her arched back, and joined a few hooks over her belly. "You do some," she said. Peck struggled to fit each tiny hook into its eye while Mona lifted her breasts. A russet nipple showed through her fingers. As Peck neared the top hook, Mona sucked in her belly and dropped her hands. Peck pulled away but Mona guided her back then raised her arms.

"Keep going."

Mona's boobs skimmed the backs of her hands, nipples puckered and tense. The leather groaned as she edged the bodice around so it faced front. Mona stretched the left cup into place.

"You do the other one."

She pulled up the leather. Mona squeezed the cups. "Do this to make sure they hold," she said as she smiled, open-mouthed, each breath loud and sweet.

Heat skittered across Peck's cheeks as Mona spun the corset back around and whipped the hooks and eyes open. Peck took the bundle into the closet and secured the lock.

Changed, she tottered into the bedroom. Her belly and her boobs bulged. Cool air came through the open hallway door. Mona's balled-up jeans and T-shirt lay on the bed. No Mona.

She staggered back in the pumps and positioned the closet door so she could peek. If she took the contraption off, Mona would talk her back into it. Besides, she wanted Mona to see her.

Mona returned five minutes later, naked. The bedroom door didn't quite catch behind her.

"Show me."

She stepped out, elbows poking her sides. The corset gave her a waist but her ribs hurt.

Mona slurped a grape drinking box until the sides collapsed. "Twirl," she said. "It's amazing. You should get one."

If she owned a corset, she could wear it under her clothes to school. A corset would make her different. In a good way. She raised her arms and stepped toward Mona.

A cheer came from downstairs.

"What's that?"

"Jim. Let's show him. He's a superb judge of what looks good."

Peck shot back into the closet and peeled off the leather without regard for the lock.

"I have to go. My dad. I forgot he was going to call."

"Are you sure? It's not late. Go get the call and come back."

"No, I'd better be there. You never know what time. His shift is unpredictable. Tonight, they might even let him off early."

When Peck emerged, Mona sat propped against the pillows in Marilyn jeans with zippers at the tapered ankles and a baby pink dotted tee with ruffled cap sleeves, organizing the singles.

The cheering had stopped when Peck passed the living room and she left calmer. At least she didn't have to witness Jim watching Mona naked.

At home, she wrapped up in a quilt and propped her feet on her headboard, toeing the edge of the Lennon banner. She winced remembering her doughy boobs cut with black leather. She didn't wear sexy clothes. That was Mona. She was Peck. Solid, square, like her name. Whatever Mona suggested, she did. She'd been moving closer to Mona when she heard Jim. She'd felt easier with Mona's body, had raised her arms for her. She burrowed into the quilt, hands in her pits. Her thighs had muscled out of the leather like Frank Furter's. Mona might have squeezed her or unhooked the corset. Legs crossed, she rubbed the seam of her jeans against the wet burn. Frank Furter could come into her bed and nuzzle between her thighs the way he had with Brad and Janet. So could Mona.

She'd worked at Venus Video only a few weeks, but she didn't want to go back. If Mona came in, she didn't know what she'd say. After she'd decided it was okay for Mona to see her in the leather clothes, Mona had left the room then come back and suggested Peck show herself to Jim. Peck wanted Mona's eyes on her only. At any reminder of a world outside that room she cringed.

She was watching *Aloha, Bobby and Rose* when Mona came into the store the next day in a denim halter with white eyelet trim, matching short shorts, and purple suede go-go boots. She'd had her hair cut close to her head on the sides and the back. Thin blades arced over her eyes.

"It's better for summer," Mona said. She put *Mary Poppins* on the counter.

Peck's hair drooped to her shoulders. She wanted to cut hers, too, now.

"It's cool," she said. "New wave." She pried open the opaque plastic box.

Only Mona could pull off such a cut. She didn't have a plain or a pretty face. She had small, even features. Her grey eyes made her skin look creamier.

In photographs, Mona transformed. What was ordinary though compelling in person turned beautiful on film.

She hoped Mona understood that they shouldn't see each

other. But maybe her own feelings were wrong. Maybe Mona acted normally and all girlfriends walked around nude together. She winced again.

Mona left without renting anything new. She didn't ask her over. She might not want to be friends anymore either.

Peck took out *Aloha, Bobby and Rose* and put on *Mary Poppins*.

That weekend she went to FastCutz and got her hair shorn on the sides and razored on top. She bought a container of pink gel with bubbles in it like ginger ale.

Mona fussed over her spikes, and Peck stopped minding when she came in the store. The following weekend Mona invited her to the mall, and she went. After that, they started Rapunzel. Peck had lost the urge to run away and had forgotten until now that she and Mona had ever dressed up in leather with Jim watching TV downstairs.

The day they met in Peck's living room, Jim Hawkes shot her a long gaze as he crossed the lawn. Maybe he knew she'd found his crime scene photographs. That she'd tried on Mona's lingerie in his bedroom while Mona rolled around nude on the black and gold satin. She took the plays home with her whenever she left Covered Wagon Trail, so he couldn't have seen them or know how she felt. She hid her feelings well, but Jim's stare worried her. That night she gathered the materials and built a model of the hall of mirrors. She wouldn't go to Mona's empty-handed again.

chapter 7

"You've got subtext. I can sense it," Joy said outside Courtroom 7-2 after my first day of testimony. I stood in a corner. She blocked me from the people craning to stare.

"I didn't add much." My chest felt torn open.

"When you looked at Ramona — and then when you wouldn't — it was clear how you felt. There must be more."

"That's why I have to come back, I guess."

"Let's go to a pub. You must be starving."

"I have plans." I was lying. I itched for the fedora. I'd just met Joy yesterday. Half a chance and I'd tell her anything she wanted.

"Ramona's no victim, Pauline. She did more than kill her husband. We should talk about what happened to you."

"I don't know about that." She'd invited me now. My blood raced.

Joy's belief in Ramona's guilt impressed me. Having been Ramona's friend had no effect on my own view. All people were capable of all things. Ramona could have killed her husband. Given the right circumstances, I could have killed Alex; or my dad, Margery. Murder happened. Murder and love. Ramona had her reasons. Finding out a friend she cared for had pursued James might move Ramona to jealous rage. Especially if she uncovered the secret after the fact, with James close at hand and the friend long gone. People did what they felt they had to do.

Alex had met me after Ramona. He might not have loved me the same if Ramona had never happened. I might have loved him more. Or not at all. But could love ever be anything but what it was? I thought so. Alex loved the best of me. Yet my other side lurked. Alex battered against it, gave up when it wouldn't budge. After making him cut me last night, I'd slunk from our bed. I'd shown him the dead part that yielded to Ramona. Then I'd deserted him. That, he'd find hard to forgive.

Joy's finger quavered on the elevator button. I wanted release from the past. This trial and this new friend gave me exactly that.

So I asked Joy to meet me back at the Buttercup Hostel. We could worry about dinner later.

I headed through Chinatown along Dundas and parked behind the Buttercup on a side street John Soules had suggested. The houses here had three storeys and scabbed brick with deep porches and turrets and lawns with century oaks and chestnuts. Once a doctors' neighbourhood, Soules had told me. On Dundas, I walked by a woman in a wheelchair with a birch leaf over her nose held in place by sunglasses. Joy waited on the Buttercup porch.

John Soules greeted Joy by name, handed me a sheet, towel, and pillowcase, and suggested Joy give me the tour. I followed her up blue-carpeted stairs past a poster of *The Scream* to a dorm room with orange walls, gold radiators, and a speckled green fireplace. A woman with pouchy cheeks and cats'-eye glasses lay smoking on a top bunk in a cardigan and gabardine slacks. She identified herself as Fern, a retired librarian from New Jersey, then rolled on her side and faced the window.

Joy flipped her hair and spoke, one shoulder raised. "I wouldn't mind staying here too, but I'd better not." Her voice made room for an invitation, but I wouldn't offer one. Whatever urge had made me hover over her in the box was gone.

After pointing out the best bed, she headed onto the balcony. She wiped the rail with a sleeve and hoisted herself up. In the bathroom, I examined my face. The skin around the dark dots of Alex's cut had reddened. When I dabbed it with wet toilet paper, it ached like a bruise. Fedora on, I dragged a plastic chair over to Joy.

"That guy, John Soules, he knew you. You've been here before?" I swabbed the seat with a towel and sat.

"A friend of mine has. And, I guess, I have too."

"Was it a guy?" My pitch veered. I'd never done girl talk well.

"A friend."

"When you ran away?"

"In the summer. We didn't stay here much, though. We stayed in squats, mostly."

"So Soules lets you hang out here now? I believe it. He's the type."

"Yup. He's helped us out a lot."

Joy traced lightning bolts on the rail. Water plunked from the roof. The sky beyond the streetlights was clear.

"He's helped you, too?"

"You know what I mean."

I didn't think I did. "Who's your friend?" I asked.

"A girl I met at Twilight Zone. She ran away a few months before me. Her dad's a dickwad who blew his back out at work and makes her help him in the toilet and stuff. It was easier for her on the street. I go with her when I need a break from my parents."

Joy took a throat lozenge tin from her jean jacket pocket and flipped the lid.

"Smoke?"

A skinny joint and half a cigarette with a pinched end rested on a white folder of rolling papers. The last time I smoked up had been months ago, with Alex.

"Soules doesn't mind?"

Joy snorted. "He'll be peeved he missed out. He'll probably stand on the sidewalk and try to catch fumes."

"Where's your friend now?" Jenna had toured the hostels of Europe last summer before her teaching job in Bratislava. I'd taken one trip, to the East Coast with Alex, and had never stayed in a motel or a hotel, let alone a hostel. This one felt like summer camp with drugs.

"She just got her own place," Joy said, her lips leaking smoke. "When I finish school, I might move in with her. My parents don't know yet."

"It must be expensive." I nipped the roach. If I got a place in Toronto, I wouldn't have to go home and have Alex look at me, my story told, with anything less than love. "How does she afford it?"

"She's a working girl," Joy said. "I told you."

"I don't know what you mean."

"She's a hooker. It sucks. But she's stopping and it beats what she had." Her words were speeding up. Maybe there was no friend and Joy was the hooker.

Then Joy said, "I've done it a few times. It's no big deal. Mostly BJs. Sometimes the johns can't get it up so we talk. It's all an act, anyway. I don't use my real name."

She made hooking sound mundane, almost appealing. I wondered if I could do it, if I'd have to in order to live down here. Joy had to deal with it that way, create an alias, make it friendly, so she could stand herself. I knew what that was like.

"What name do you use?"

"Trista. It's corny. Like sadness in French. Ha ha."

"The opposite of you."

"Hardly. My friend uses Aimee. Loved one. It suits her. You

could do it, too. It's easy money. All cash. What about your name? John called you Peck. Does everyone call you that?"

"No. Maybe my parents when I was a kid." When she said "easy money, all cash," I pictured my face near some man's dirty penis. I couldn't do it. I felt sad for her the way I had for K, though Joy was different. Something in her made it okay to do what should have disgusted her. I understood now why I'd liked her immediately.

"You said a lot today," Joy said. "You must feel tired."

"I feel free." *Scared, too. Scared like never before.* I wedged my hands between my thighs.

"I would find it hard to testify against my lover."

My breath stopped. She said "lover" so readily, like "boyfriend," or "toaster."

"But we weren't," I said, too loudly. "Lovers, I mean." Alex had said "lover," too. I squared my shoulders and sat wide-kneed. My jeans dipped into a puddle.

"On the stand you said you were. During Rapunzel. It's fine."

"We played and flirted and tried on clothes together — but as friends, not lovers. That's what I saw." I pointed my toes, let the pot smoke syrup my bones.

"Sounds like you were wrong, Pauline."

"Maybe, but I'm the one telling what happened. The truth."

"It's only the truth as you see it."

"How else can I see it? And how can I know it was real, or make it real, if I don't tell it?"

"If it happened," Joy said, "it's real."

"A person loses faith."

"That it happened?"

"That. And that it is happening. That I am who I am." My tongue spelled "am" on the roof of my mouth.

"It's clear to me," Joy said. "Who you are."

"Shh. Don't spoil the surprise."

At 10:45 p.m., after Joy left, I called home on the payphone outside the basement den where John Soules and a greying black man in a vest and jeans watched *Hockey Night in Canada* under flashing red Christmas lights. Alex didn't answer, and I counted the beeps at the end of the outgoing message to see how many people had called before I hung up without a word.

By 10:45 p.m., Alex was usually home, showered, shaved, and drinking a frosty beer in the living room. Then again, so was I.

I took the bunk furthest from Fern the Librarian's snores. The comforter smelled like scalp. Tonight I'd sleep alone. I hadn't seen my dad since convocation two years ago. He'd driven over to Guelph from Cloud Lake. Afterward, I met him under the browning trees outside War Memorial Hall. He'd cut his curls close and had some grey around his ears and in his beard. He had a beard. We walked across the field to the parking lot behind the university. I wore a two-piece jade dress with buckled green suede shoes. He told me about moose season and deer season and made Haliburton sound like the centre of the world. He would move there, he said, but for Apco. He had three ladies — he called them ladies. Only one was married. She was the one he'd marry if he could.

He said, "Your mother went here, for a year. Did you know?"

"I didn't."

"For Home Ec."

"They joke about that. To get their M.R.S. degrees."

"Not her. It was her father's idea. She wanted to travel, be an artist. The alternative was business college. She couldn't type."

Margery had kept her drawings between two boards tied with ribbon. Buildings, mostly, but some people, too. She had shown me one of her mother, a young woman with short, thumb-smudged hair.

"She looks younger than you," I'd said. We were at the kitchen table. I leaned my head on my arm.

"That's how old she was." Her mother had died before I was born. Nobody had told me when.

"How old were you when you drew the photo," I said.

"Picture." She didn't look at me. "Not much older than you."

At eight I drew people with their arms sticking out straight from their bodies. I imagined how sad I would feel if my mother died. I turned on my side and moped. She cupped my shoulder. I didn't move. She didn't usually hug. I wished she would.

"You do what you can, kid. You have a good father. That, I never got. There's the difference."

She'd stood and walked out. She'd left us before the year was up.

I strained to remember her portfolio. Had it gone with her? Had we moved it to Cloud Lake? My heels brought up divots from the path as my dad and I approached Johnston Hall. Mud soaked the suede and chilled my instep.

"I never heard from her," my dad said with tiny hope.

"Me either."

I didn't miss having a mother as much as I missed my mother herself. If she showed up now, because of the trial, I'd take care of her, here, at the Buttercup, at home in Flats Mills, or wherever she lived. If my mother showed up now, I wouldn't let her out of my sight.

The last time I saw my dad, James Hawkes had two weeks to live. My dad had liked him; Ramona, too. I wondered if he remembered them now. He hadn't called about Ramona being in the news, so maybe not.

I read over the police statement and turned to my notebook. I'd filled almost half since the police interview. "There's more to this story," Joy had said. Detective Stanton had said that, too. I made notes about that day at the South Simcoe Police Station.

Detective Young had ejected the cassette. Stanton had left the room and brought back a manila envelope that he emptied on the pocked table.

Photographs scattered, square and rectangular, murky and bright. Photos from different cameras taken in different years. Limpid Polaroids with white borders. Textured surfaces with rounded corners. Dates in red. A few, not many, black and white. I stared at the heap of colours and light without registering the images.

Stanton gathered up the pile and held it out. When I didn't take it, he dropped it on my lap.

"Look at them, Pauline," he said. "It may be difficult, but it's crucial that you go through all of them. Tell us if you recognize even a lamp or a piece of furniture. Or if something reminds you of something else. We need to know."

Young stayed at the table with me while Stanton paced by the door.

The first photo, a Polaroid, shows the short nude torso of a girl, arms raised, the skin like white paint against the dark background. There are new breasts and a modest amount of curly hair. I flipped through the others and found similar poses, no faces, though several photos show a whole body with a towel or blanket covering the head. Some have long hair, wavy brown, straight blonde. There are moles, warts, freckles, scabs, bruises, scratches, scars. A line of down bisecting a belly. A butterfly drawn in purple magic marker. Spread legs, flung-out arms. In most, grey carpet, sometimes a yellow and brown afghan, a brown towel, a yellow pillowcase. One has almost no breasts. Orange freckles splatter her skin. Several photos feature the same body, tanned all over, with no bikini triangles. This one has the best figure and poses more than the others, back arched, ribs high. This body is languid, the others merely prone.

It was easy, after I got used to what I was seeing, to recognize the tanned body. Though I'd never looked at it straight, laid out before me, like a lover's, or my own, and couldn't say how I figured out its identity. I just knew.

I examined the others, not sure what I could tell. I hadn't seen many girls without clothes, only centrefolds, murder victims, and myself — and I'd never looked that closely there. I checked the stack again, only half aware, and there it was, a thin matte photo, the square body on grey carpet, the brown and yellow afghan over the face, the shiny black fringe against the neck. The high breasts, solid belly and hips, skin as white as the overexposed skin in the first photograph, dark flecks clustered on the chest.

"This one is me."

Detective Young left and came back with another tape.

"The final witness might be a letdown after this," Stanton said, lighting a cigarette but not offering one.

"Who's that?"

"The star witness, the last of Ramona's friends to testify. Your story is supposed to lead up to hers. She's savvy and, even better, she's young."

I tilted my chin.

"Relatively speaking, that is," Stanton said. He took the cassette from Young and picked at its plastic wrapper. "Lucy's seventeen."

Young shot him a look. "Wha-at?" said Stanton.

"Her name?"

"Right. Sorry about that. Pauline won't tell, will you?" Sheepish, he chewed his cheek and shrugged. I shrugged back. Obviously I told whatever I liked.

While Young put the cassette in the player, Stanton started. "You said Ramona invited you to stay overnight. Can you tell us more?"

Young placed the silver machine in front of me. I swallowed twice and sipped my water, and when she pressed "record" and "play," I talked. I'd needed few prompts after that.

At the Buttercup, I didn't turn off the overhead light. The police statement made no mention of the star witness being a letdown after me. No mention of Lucy at all. Seventeen, Lucy might be the one alleging sexual assault. Her name would be withheld. Stanton had slipped up. Though he did have me pegged — I was important, to Ramona and to the case — but I controlled how much I told. I'd have to keep my ego out of the way. My head grew warm and I brooded, bound, now more than ever, to Ramona's fate. I wished she would go away.

Nobody else came in, and Fern snored, oblivious, as I wrote the story down. I returned to my dad. He was all I had then.

At Foodplex, Hank trundled the cart around the aisles and pronounced on the ingredients of a proper sleepover. Peck slunk behind.

"How would you know, Dad?"

"I have friends. Girlfriends."

"That's for sure."

"I want you to have a good time, Peck. You don't get enough of those."

He bought Pop-Tarts and 1/2 Moons, marshmallows, diet pop, and pudding cups. In the checkout line he added three beauty magazines and two tabloids.

"Dad, you're such a girl."

"I wouldn't go that far," he said.

Peck stopped him from going into Super Drug for makeup.

"Mona's got all that," she said.

"Well, remember you are a guest," he said. "Don't abuse the situation."

chapter 8

Hank dropped her off at 17 Covered Wagon Trail with enough to feed the entire engagement party. He trailed behind her up the walk, but as the door opened, she turned, kissed him on the cheek, and slugged his arm.

He swaggered backward to the car.

"If you need me," he said, "call Susan's parents. I left the number in the side pocket."

He waved as he drove off.

"His girlfriend lives with her parents?" Mona asked. She lifted the duffel bag, eyebrows perked. Peck followed her inside.

"She lives in a cabin near Kashag and with her parents down here. They go there a lot. "

"He's met her parents. Promising. How old?"

"I haven't met them."

"Her. Have you met her?"

"She's twenty-six."

"A younger woman. Do you think they'll get married?"

"Oh my God, I hope not. He's still married, I think," Peck said. She didn't mention the ladies she sometimes found lounging on the couch in Hank's velour bathrobe.

Mona plopped the bag on the spare bed.

"Why so heavy?"

Peck unpacked the new play and the hall of mirrors model before Mona could mention the party. The distraction worked. As usual, Mona dismissed the dialogue, but the model got her attention. They moved into the master bedroom and the play took hold.

The second time through, the crone led the princess to the prince's domain. The crone eased her body onto the floor of the unlit den. The bride tucked up her gowns and followed suit. The TV glowed ultramarine blue. The crone pressed a button and spun a knob.

Grainy trunks and branches jounced past. Footsteps crunched leaves and sticks. There was no score, but another sound droned in and out. Then the shadows lightened, as if a flashlight had switched on. A woman with long blonde hair in a sleeveless minidress dashed in front of the camera. She wove, ducked under branches, batted her forearms against trunks. The camera waited then moved with her. She turned back, her face swollen, blotchy, and Peck recognized the other sound. The woman was screaming. Blood and scratches latticed her skin from the assault of the dense trees. Was she trying to escape? The woman could see the camera. She'd looked at it. None of this was real if a camera was there. Frantic, she stumbled and dodged. Panting punctuated the screams, whose ragged, tearing quality constricted the chest. A dim, heavy figure crashed out of the woods from behind the camera and fell upon the blonde. Her cries muffled briefly then resumed full force and the screen went blank.

"He's here."

"That's him?"

"His car. He's home."

"But that. Was that?"

Mona turned off the TV and stood up.

"Let's get the party stuff out," she said.

Jim came in the side door and Mona hugged him from the stairs. He twinkled at Peck. After a glance at Mona, he offered Peck a hug, too.

She hung back, unable to shake the hall of mirrors' demon brides and the woman in the woods.

"Hey," Jim said. "We're friends here."

Mona nodded, so Peck gave herself up to Jim's clutch. His breath heated her neck. The screams of the girl in the forest jabbed at her. She pulled away.

She had seen movies like *The Texas Chainsaw Massacre* and *Doctor Butcher*. Venus Video had many, and though she wasn't supposed to, she played them in the store. This one had looked more like TV than a movie and the girl like a real person. Surely Mona didn't connect the movie to Jim. He had interrupted their game by accident. He was a normal, friendly man. Hail fellow well met, as Hank said about the Sergeant.

"I'm going to barbecue," Jim said. "Then you girls can plan without having to worry about anything else."

Peck and Mona lounged on the patio with notebooks, pens, and a stack of bridal magazines. Mona wore Marilyn jeans and a black ripped T-shirt with the white face of Siouxsie Sioux. Peck shivered in her Malamutes tee and jean shorts. Thunder growled but no rain came. She sipped a wine spritzer, made lists, and considered whether to mention true crime to Jim. When Jim asked if she liked her steak medium, tough, or bloody, Mona's knee touched hers and she pushed against it.

"Tough," she said. Mona grinned.

Jim disappeared after he'd rinsed the dishes and stacked them in the dishwasher. Peck and Mona lingered outside until the mosquitoes got too bad then moved their lists to the kitchen table. The TV muttered in the den. Peck hoped Jim hadn't noticed which tape they'd been playing.

Near midnight, he came back in and poured three glasses of wine, not spritzers.

"Take a break, girls."

"We can't," Mona said.

"You've got her tomorrow. She can come back."

"All right. Let's go."

Peck followed them into the den and leaned with a cushion against the bookshelf. Jim set the wine on the TV then sat next to Mona on the couch. The radio played Bon Jovi, "Shot through the heart, and you're to blame."

Jim swept his arm at the true crime books looming over Peck.

"Mona mentioned you had an interest," he said.

"I read those books, sure. My mother used to. Then I started." She didn't tell him she hadn't read one since she'd moved to Westwoods.

"You can borrow mine any time you want, Peck. I've got them all. What's interesting about my approach is not that I study serial killers from a legal standpoint, which I have done. One must. What I do is attempt to become them."

He tightened his arm around Mona.

"So you wouldn't —" Peck said.

"Of course not, but I research them and experience as much as I can. I read what they read, eat what they eat, wear what they wear. I've tried to acquire as many of their weapons as possible. I listen to their music and attempt to bring myself to their state of mind when they killed. Well, on the brink of when they killed."

"On breaks, he locks himself in for hours, days even, to get into the role."

"I pick one of them, like Albert DeSalvo, and I memorize his line of thinking, his circumstances, his grievances, his moods. As best I can, using accounts of those who knew him, I study his walk, his build, his manner of talking. I work on an accent. His was Boston, so it took some work, but I got it. Like a method actor. I recreate the days leading up to his crime. Then I take myself through it."

"She gets it. She knows what it's like."

"I even go out into the world when I'm in this place. With

Mona's help, I recreate the encounter, with minimal violence and no murder, of course."

"Then he stops."

"That's right, babe. I always stop before it gets out of hand. I take things up to that line that separates me from them. I ride that edge of sanity. Of murder. It'll make me a better lawyer, that's a given. And a better person. I'm not only aware of what we are all capable of, which is good for a lawyer who's going into the area I've chosen. But it helps me as a person to embrace the realm of possibility. I'm more open, and I appreciate what it's like to be sane."

"Isn't it hard to stop yourself once you go that far?" Peck asked.

Jim paused for one beat then said, "Of course not. I've got exceptional self-control. I know what I'm doing at all times, and I'm clear on my reasons for doing it. I have an agenda, a program, like these guys do, only mine doesn't include the compulsion to kill."

"Only to experience it," Peck said. A commercial for a stereo store came on. Mona switched off the radio and put on a Van Halen tape.

"Right. Though I can't experience it exactly. I'd have to kill someone, and I'm not prepared to do that. That would be wrong, and frankly I'd be too detached, too objective. I'd also have it all planned out, expecting it to happen as it did with whichever guy it is that I'm playing, and it wouldn't. Each murder is unique. Like making love. Each person you make love with, it's different. You can only murder someone once, so the encounter is powerful. You can't plan what will occur between you and your victim, and I'm not prepared for that randomness. I need control, and I have no reason to kill other than to understand killing from the serial murderer's perspective."

"You could shoot someone. Then you'd know what's going to happen."

"Not entirely. You don't know, with 100 percent certainty, if the gun will work or if you'll aim accurately or if the victim will move. You can practise and practise and have even 99 percent certainty, but there is always an element of risk. And I'm not interested in risk."

"So you act out every part up to that."

"I do."

"He does," Mona said. "It's amazing. You wouldn't believe it. Maybe you would. I can feel the psychopath in him taking over. He turns into a whole other person."

"It's not in me any more than it's in anyone else."

"True," said Mona. "But you have to admit it's more well-developed in you. Or rather, you've allowed it more room. You're more accepting of expressing that side of yourself."

"That's it," Jim said. "Everyone has that side. Everyone. I don't care who you're talking about. Even your Mother Teresas. Your Gandhis. Most repress it. I'm not advocating that everyone get out there and explore their inner murderer. I'm saying —"

"That it's there," Peck said.

"Right. I've chosen to use it to study the area of my fascination. Not everyone could handle it." .

"Mona could."

Jim and Mona stared at Peck. Mona tipped the last drops of the bottle into her glass.

"You're right. Mona can handle it." Jim's voice mellowed as he added, "You might even be able to, Peck."

Mona left the room but not before locking eyes with Peck with the gaze of the princess she'd left behind hours ago locked in the curse of the crone.

"No matter what, of course, Mona is a partner, in the true sense of the word, because she gets it, she understands. That's why I'm marrying her."

This last he declared as Mona entered carrying a new bottle of wine. She handed a full glass to Peck.

"This is some of the good stuff we're considering for the wedding. Tell me what you think."

Mona passed the bottle to Jim along with a corkscrew.

"We'll have our usual," she said. She snuggled in beside him as he peeled the seal and spiralled the worm into the cork.

As a surprise, Jim had movies.

He put *Fun with Dick and Jane* into the VCR and fiddled with the remote. Peck excused herself and went to the spare room. When she came back, a bag of snacks dangling from each hand, the movie was playing. Jim had slid onto his back and held Mona's waist as they kissed. Peck rustled the bags then emptied them in a heap. She sat on the floor, her back to the smooching, unwrapped a 1/2 Moon, and watched George Segal lose his job.

The couch creaked, and she tuned Jim and Mona out. Hank and his girlfriends made more noise. She should leave them alone. Go to the bedroom. Or home, even.

Her mind leapt from topic to topic. Everything else fuzzed. The wedding wine was cold and drops coated the glass head. She downed most of it and gobbled three 1/2 Moons.

DeSalvo was the one. The Boston Strangler. Thirteen kills in the 1960s, Hank's era. She pictured Jim acting out DeSalvo. What would that feel like? Could she act with him? What had DeSalvo done? She remembered a nightgown. A woman in bed. Pantyhose tied in a bow. Didn't DeSalvo —? She closed her eyes to get it more clearly. Didn't he rape? Before or after he killed? Did it matter? Yes, it mattered. Very much. Because if it was after.

Jim wouldn't. Jim said he didn't kill. He said no violence. And rape was violence.

But it wouldn't be rape if Mona agreed to let him do it.

Or if she did.

She blinked as Jane yelled at Dick. This Jane Fonda had dark hair, not blonde like the one in *Cat Ballou*. There must be two Jane Fondas. Her eyelids sank. The kissing noises had stopped. She arched her eyebrows. Her glass tilted dangerously, so she raised it and swallowed the rest. With care, she placed it on a shelf. She peered at the movie. Then her head drooped and her eyes closed for good.

She woke with a perpendicular neck, cricks in her shoulders and knees, and an afghan swathing her middle. She thrashed free. Mona slumped against Jim, both asleep, the TV off. Snacks and wrappers littered the carpet. Birds clacked outside.

She cradled the blanket on her way to the bathroom. Goo clogged her eyelids. A viscous taffy dragged her muscles. She landed on the toilet lid without pulling down her shorts and flopped forward. Later, she dragged the blanket into the spare room. She fell on the bed, the blanket bunched under one arm. She ground her face into the pillow and didn't open her eyes again until afternoon.

chapter 9

The next morning I came awake kicking at the Buttercup Hostel. A streetcar purred below the open window. The radiator gurgled. The orange walls and sunflower prints looked oddly cheerless in the morning light. I'd slept face up, elbows crooked, fists bunched. It hurt to lick my dry mouth. Yesterday, I'd had a sense of adventure. Like Jenna in Europe, I was a traveller staying at a hostel. Today I felt fugitive.

Mentioning DeSalvo had been like hitting the detectives with a fine drug. Their attention, their hunger, had made telling the story easier. Detective Stanton had wanted to know what happened and how I felt. He'd said the Crown would have a tricky time using how I felt in court, but knowing helped the lawyers form their questions.

Ramona's role had interested the detectives most. Had James coerced Ramona? Had she feared for her life if she didn't comply? Or had Ramona been willing? The Crown would likely ask me these questions on the stand today. I burrowed under the smelly pillow. My loyalties were definitely shifting.

A week before the trial began, Ron Laurie and Detective Stanton had prepped me at a Brampton police station. Ron opened our morning interview by commenting on my attitude. He sat with his back to the sunny window, his eyes in shadow. I frowned.

"Your perspective. Your point of view. How you chose to see things." He was certain, he said, that I could make him understand.

"I don't know what you're talking about," I said. I'd told my story clearly. Anybody could figure it out. Detective Stanton hadn't had a problem with it. He stood in the corner now, chewing on a toothpick. I guessed he'd given up smoking.

"The video," he said. "James Hawkes's plan to act out serial killings. I don't understand why you didn't react. I don't understand your attitude."

"I was eighteen," I said. "Don't you remember being eighteen?" At eighteen, what I wanted mattered, not what was right or wrong. I felt judged now, a stupid girl. I wished Detective Young had shown up for this one, cold as she was. Though doubtless at eighteen, she'd have run right to her parents the moment Ramona told her how she met James.

"Weren't you born in the fall? That's what I have down here. September 1."

"Whatever. I guess I was seventeen. No big deal. Nothing happened then."

Detective Stanton sat and took out his notebook.

"When I read your police statement," Ron said, "I pulled out the murder victim's collection of pornography. A regular porn hound, that guy. One after another, I slapped tapes into the VCR. I'd already watched them all and assumed James Hawkes had purchased the grainier prints on the black market. Police never found a video camera."

"That doesn't mean there wasn't one," I said. Detective Stanton shot me a look and sucked in the corner of his mouth. I didn't care. Ron made me cocky.

"We're not trying to undermine you, Pauline," Detective Stanton said. "We need you comfortable on the stand, but we don't need any surprises. Get your anger out now, that's fine, but stick to the story on the stand."

I nodded, happy to get a reaction.

Ron continued. "None of the women in the films resemble any of the girls Ramona befriended. Nobody has recognized them. If I showed you, you'd see a pattern in the scenes, women chased, women captured, women bound, women struggling. Most are obviously actresses, their faces made up paler than the rest of their bodies, but the occasional one seems ungainly and lost. Like she's not acting. The sun was coming up and I'd already fast-forwarded through more than ten tapes when I found her. The screaming blonde in the woods from your story."

I knew what he was getting at. He had made a connection.

"You said none of this is real, Pauline, if the camera is there," Detective Stanton said through his toothpick. "We have it on tape. I watched that blonde scramble through the brush, too. We could put the video in now and we could all watch it together. If that babe's torn cries and scored arms weren't real, I don't know what is."

"Maybe that's it. Maybe you don't know what is real." I dug a nail into the table.

"Did you not entertain the possibility that she wasn't acting?" Ron's cheeks glared. "Did it not occur to you that she could be a real victim of exactly the kind of event James Hawkes claimed he liked to stage?"

"Why would it? He said he only did things with Ramona."

"And you believed him."

"Yes."

If I believed anything, I had to believe everything.

Sprawled on the Buttercup bunk, I stroked the scratch. A charge dropped into my belly, shot down my thighs. The torturers in S&M books repelled me. There was no love in that prick the Marquis de Sade. What word caught my own desire up? Masochism, maybe, without the sado. Krafft-Ebing coined the term in his *Psychopathia Sexualis* to express a perversion. In dictionaries, it meant gratification from pain and degradation inflicted by another. Self-denial was part of it, too, though if anything, it indulged a self that wanted the pain that articulated love. Leopold von Sacher-Masoch, the term's unwitting namesake, had written, "My love for you is part hatred, part fear." I liked that. He'd also written, "I want to be able to worship a woman, and I can only do so if she is cruel to me." Awe flared, and I hooked a nail under my scab's crust. Alex's cut stemmed from an urge in me no less alive for its wrongness. I couldn't go home now.

I opted out of the Buttercup's coffee-doughnut combo and wandered along Dundas in search of a newspaper box. I read the *Telstar* over a greasy breakfast at a diner called Mossy's next to a boxing gym. Cynthia Fist had written about me in her column. I felt exposed, as if I were overhearing gossip about myself. Thousands of people would see what she wrote. Anybody interested in the case — Alex, maybe my dad — would know what had happened to me. Climbing up a statue on University Avenue naked and shouting my story through a bullhorn would feel more private. Ron advised against looking at the news, but I studied Cynthia Fist's column, convinced I wanted to understand the Crown's line of thinking. I really wanted praise, some evidence of support. I didn't find it.

Life after "the murderess"
By Cynthia Fist
Toronto Telstar

Toronto – This one has me baffled, folks, I don't mind saying. Pauline Brown is not like the other witnesses, who at least showed a spark. Some engagement with the world. Life after befriending a murderess.

This one is stale. Her voice is a dull monotone. Her face is plastic, her shoulders droop, and her hands lie limp in her lap. She is a doll on a shelf. I would doubt she was living except that her lips move when she speaks. Barely. And what does she say?

She has had a life since this friendship. Her husband is an intern and she says she's a writer. This much we know.

But she is curious. There but not there. Damaged. It's disturbing. A contrast to the peppy Lyndsey Franklin. Ron Laurie is going around and around with her.

Creepy as she is, I'm glad he's bringing her back. Now maybe we'll hear the truth. Could she be a victim of a different sort than the others? A turning point in Ramona Hawkes's fledgling career? We'll have to wait and see.

Unbelievable. Nobody had ever called me "creepy" or "stale." Was I deadpan? Vacant? Joy didn't think so. Or maybe she did. Maybe everybody did. The line "she says she is a writer" bothered me most. As if I weren't. As if I hadn't written all those murder stories and spent years outlining the novel about the runaway ghost. Though, who was I kidding. Other than the background of my sordid past with Ramona, I'd written hardly a word worth showing. But no "spark"? No "engagement with the world"? "Dull monotone"? "Plastic"? I sounded like a monster. That, I refused to believe. Fuck her.

I dropped ten dollars on the table, more than twice the price of the breakfast, and walked back to the hostel. I dumped the paper in the trash, but I didn't feel any better.

I leaned against the wall outside Courtroom 7-2. On Ron's advice, I'd dressed up in a brown skort with matching tights, patent leather pumps, white blouse, and black rayon blazer, all borrowed from Fern, my ponytail clipped with her pewter thistle barrette. No makeup. Wisps framed my face, but up close anyone might see the hairline scratch. Detective Stanton approached with a woman.

"This is Pauline," he said. "Pauline, Cynthia Fist."

"Call me Cindy," Cynthia said.

She was plumper than her picture, with a slash of a face. Her red lips matched her frames. Yesterday, she'd bustled into the courtroom, jokey, talking. She'd clapped the arms and shoulders of the other reporters, mostly men over forty.

"Good to meet you in person," she said, hand extended. I didn't take it. "Two days on the stand. What you're doing takes courage."

"It's not like I have a choice."

Stanton stood at ease. He folded his lips into a line and blinked at me.

"It's hard enough to remember," Cindy said. "But to talk about it at a trial? I can't imagine. I hope you've got some support here." She glanced at Stanton. I caught a whiff of Opium.

"Nope, no support. Perhaps I'm too creepy."

"Pauline, you're not creepy. I see that. It's the trauma of the situation, it's gotten to you. You're probably more sensitive than — more traumatized. Listen, why don't you let me take you for coffee? I'm a good ear. It can make a difference."

"What, do you think I'm an idiot, on top of everything else? Detective Stanton, shouldn't you be protecting me from wingnuts like this, so my testimony's not affected? Sheesh." I pursed my lips and glared at him. Cindy watched him, too. He ignored us both.

"Pauline, I'm a reporter," she said. "I put down what I see. Did you notice, I wrote about how curious you've made me? How I feel you might be the key to Ramona's crime? There's something about you. Not many people know, but I'm doing a book on this trial. An important one, from a woman's point of view. We could work together, get the real story down."

"I said it all on the stand. Leave me alone and keep your creepy observations to yourself. That's all the support I need. Excuse me." I stepped around her and headed for the bathroom.

"I'm here every day," she called. "You know where to find me. Maybe I'll try you at home?"

"Good luck to you," I muttered.

At 10:12 a.m. on my second day of testimony, I made my way to the stand. A lion and a unicorn reared on the royal coat of arms above Justice Larraby. *Dieu et mon droit*, read a banner at the bottom. I remembered these from Canadian History. God and my right. The other motto was written on a garter, *Honi soit qui mal y pense*. Evil to him who evil thinks.

On the verge, the story clogged my chest like a lump of pulsating grey meat. It thrust against my tonsils. I fought it down.

White noise fed the room. Air blew. Voices blended. I bent the microphone, took in the wood-panelled walls. The expectant jury. Ramona. During the trial, her almond complexion had drained. Her blonde hair, darkened, clung to her skull. Her grey eyes had retreated. I scanned the gallery. Joy sat in front. Other faces I'd seen in the lineup yesterday, many in the same spots.

The back door opened and in came a man in a tan bomber jacket and striped shirt. The back row made room. He wore brassy frames, but the rest looked the same. The beard, the curls.

My dad. I bent my left thumb back like a gear shift. I didn't want him to watch me. I wanted him to find out what happened afterward, in the news, like everyone else. He sat far enough away that I couldn't meet his eyes. He faced me, though. Everybody did. I felt trapped, exhilarated. Somebody here loved me.

I joined my hands on my lap. My hairline itched. The memories flickered like movies, the way they did when I was writing. With my dad there, I let go of Pauline and slipped into Peck. I added details, changed dialogue, moved events. The clothes, the hair — the more I shaped the story, the less it contained me.

Nobody called me on it so I let it rip.

Excerpt from Transcript
RAMONA HAWKES
v

HER MAJESTY THE QUEEN:

April 22, 1992
Toronto, Ontario

MR. LAURIE:	What changed in your friendship with the accused after that?
MS. BROWN:	What we did together, or rather how we did it. Where we went with it. And sometimes James was involved.
MR. LAURIE:	How did Mr Hawkes's involvement change things?
MS. BROWN:	It was good and bad. He was an intruder on our world, and he threatened my bond with Ramona. But I did like the closeness it gave me with him.
MR. LAURIE:	How did the accused respond to this closeness you had with her fiancé?
MS. BROWN:	She encouraged it.
MR. LAURIE:	Why would she do that?
MR. WITHERSON:	Objection, Your Honour. My friend is asking for

	speculation.
MR. LAURIE:	It's not speculation, Your Honour, if the accused spoke to the witness about her motivation.
THE COURT:	Proceed with care.
MR. LAURIE:	Yes, Your Honour. Ms. Brown, what did the accused say to you about including James?
MS. BROWN:	She said it would be good for her relationship with her fiancé, that it would bring them closer together.
MR. LAURIE:	Specifically, what did she suggest would bring them closer together?
MS. BROWN:	Role-playing with me. She said it was her idea and James was enthusiastic. They wanted me to agree.
MR. LAURIE:	How did you respond?
MS. BROWN:	I didn't agree right away. I didn't want to give up what I had with Ramona. We wouldn't be able to do the fairy tales anymore. James was too old, and a man, so why would he? Plus we'd had that conversation about serial murderers and James's practice of role-playing the killers. That was the kind of role-playing they were talking about. After that night I stayed over I learned that Ramona created more intense scenes with James than she ever had with me. And if I wanted to keep up, I'd have to become part of it. Ramona encouraged me.
MR. LAURIE:	How did she do that?
MS. BROWN:	She was my friend. She thought people should just try things. I did, too, because she did. And James liked me. Ramona told me how much he respected my intelligence and knowledge, how smart and interesting he thought I was for someone my age. Everything she'd said about me before was now repeated as something James had observed.
MR. LAURIE:	How did your relationship with Mr. Hawkes develop?
MS. BROWN:	I don't know. It just did.
MR. LAURIE:	What did you have in common with Mr. Hawkes?
MS. BROWN:	Murder books, I guess. The serial killer thing.
MR. LAURIE:	How was your relationship with Mr. Hawkes different from your relationship with the accused?

MS. BROWN: I felt like his friend, but not the way I felt it with Ramona. There was no bond with James. I liked that he thought so well of me and I wanted to hear what he had to say.

MR. LAURIE: What caused you finally to give in and role-play with the couple?

MS. BROWN: Withdrawal. And jealousy. Ramona wouldn't act out the plays alone with me anymore. And I knew what she was doing with James. They didn't talk about it much. On weekends and holidays, I wouldn't hear from her. I felt left out. I was angry at them. And then one day a long time later, at the end of Christmas holidays, I was so bored and lonely that I went over.

MR. LAURIE: And after that?

MS. BROWN: After that I participated.

chapter 10

The morning of Labour Day Saturday, Peck settled into the sun-warmed Ranger. Hank punched in a Loretta Lynn tape, and they drove north out of Westwoods and east to the 400 Highway. She clenched her shoulders against the old despair of her mother leaving. Identical houses melted and onion and corn fields made way for pine trees and lakes. Then, surprise. Loretta was singing, "You ain't woman enough," and hope washed in at those first pink speckled rocks festooned with sprayed white initials cradled by hearts. Peck surged with what she would later describe as home.

At the Salters' Burt and two hounds were tied to doghouses nestled under a pine grove. Mrs. Salter informed her that Malcolm had fought with the Sergeant and had moved into the Kendalls' basement, two houses down.

In her slicker and duck boots, Peck crouched beside Burt. No matter where she put her hands or what she said, Burt wouldn't stop moving. The Sergeant's hounds bayed to announce Malcolm's approach through the wet trees.

"Hey Peckdog."

"I Dig a Malcolm."

He'd had his shag trimmed into a pointy spray with a rat tail on the left. A plastic headband caught back her own growing-out layers. "Your guy acts more regal than these plebeian hounds," Malcolm said.

He squatted and stroked Burt's head with a flat hand. Burt gazed back, eyewhites showing. His body jiggled and his tongue flapped against his chin.

"He wasn't like this before," Peck said. "Don't tell him, but I'm afraid he's turning into one of these brainless bozohounds."

"So take him back with you."

"I want to. How's that trailer, by the way?" She flicked his drenched sleeve.

"Why don't you come and see. The rentals are going to a dance after dinner. Tell them you want to stay home. I'll meet you in there."

After Hank had left with the Salters for the arena, Peck drove the Ranger along the Pike River Road toward Kashag town. Rain and pine gum made the road tacky. Brown wishbone pine needles clung to the windshield. At the next line, she took a left and drove in a square until she was heading back down the Pike River Road. She coasted past her old house just north of the Salters'. Green lattice surrounded the white porch. Ruffled curtains hung in the windows. A Jeep sat in the driveway. She'd moved just three months ago, yet the house had gone strange. She sped up and hung a sharp left onto the Salters' springy sand driveway.

"Strawberry Peck Forever," Malcolm said when she closed the trailer door. His high-tops sat unlaced under the table. He'd set up Monopoly. She was relieved. She'd hardly thought about him over the summer and didn't think she could kiss him again.

"Being for the Benefit of Mr. Malcolm."

"I brought in the beer. We should probably forego our tour

of Mike's murder album and the various other delights of the Salter household."

They lay together on the top bunk. Rain rattled the skylight like ice cubes.

"How much do you know about murderers, anyway?" she asked.

"Some. The Sergeant thinks he's an expert," Malcolm said. He tapped his fingers on the ceiling.

"Him? I guess he could be."

"He's not. He knows surveillance. He can tell you anything you want about how to watch somebody without them knowing. But actual murderers? The Sergeant's not your man."

"Do you know anything about the Boston Strangler?"

"Sure. Everybody knows that guy. He liked to choke old ladies with their pantyhose." Malcolm rolled on his side and traced her throat. His legs bent, his feet dangled over the edge.

"Why do you think we like looking at those pictures? Why do we want to know about the Boston Strangler?"

He blew on her collarbone. "Everybody reads that stuff," he said. His hand edged under her waistband. She pulled it away.

"I think there's more. What about people who read it all the time? People who try to do the things in those books."

"They're sick. But no sicker than us. We looked at *Hustler*, too. If the Sergeant knew, he'd arrest us."

"You'd like that, wouldn't you, Savoy Malcolm."

"I do believe I would."

Sunday morning, Hank stood at the kitchen window in his bathrobe and moccasins. He moved aside for her. Burt lay in a hump on a mud hill. If she went out, the hounds' carolling would wake the house.

"He chains them when they're pups, Dad. They only go free during hunting season."

"It's no wonder his dogs run off."

"Why does he even name them?"

Peck asked again about bringing Burt to Westwoods. Hank relented.

"If you take full responsibility. We're not in the country now."

She fingered his sleeve and let his hand find hers. She smiled up into his smile and told herself it would be all right. Burt would adapt.

After school, Peck took Burt on hour-long walks. As the days got colder and night fell earlier, the walks fed her plays. With Burt's rump swinging before her, she figured out the characters, their relationships, and what happened. She tested every possibility before she decided on the words, the hardest part. She could only tell what happened to her characters through what they said, so she had to get the words right. With Burt leading her forward in the rising dusk, she wrote four new plays, mediocre variations on her killer fiancé idea.

Mona read each one and tossed it aside.

"You can do better."

Lunch hours in the library, Peck thought about Jim and Mona acting out criminals. She found the true crimes at the bottom of a paperback carousel. She skimmed paragraphs and flipped past photos. She needed a crime with a role for Jim. If Jim wanted to do it, Mona would. Mona was giving Jim everything he desired to keep the wedding plans rolling. Jim's character should have a female accomplice to lure the teenage girl. The two women would survive and triumph and become bonded friends.

In her new play there are three.

A man and his wife meet a seventeen-year-old hitchhiker. They offer her a ride. When the girl gets into the car, the wife shoves her to the floor, covers her with a blanket, and holds a gun to her head. They drive around for a couple of hours. Then they take the girl to their house. Before they go in, the wife leans over the seat, peels two strips of duct tape from a roll, and sticks one over the girl's mouth and one over her eyes. They stumble into the house, where they rip the tape from her eyes but not her mouth and lead her down a hall to the basement stairs, gun at her back. No lights are on, but she glimpses a kitchen, though her eye sockets throb and her lids sting.

Downstairs, the wife locks the girl into a closet with a sleeping bag. The wife's gentle hands and pleading face give the girl the idea for her plan.

Peck had a hard time with the next part. According to true crime books, couples kidnapped in order to rape and torture and then kill. She had to devise ways to maintain the intention of violence in her story without anybody ever having to act on it. Maybe the hitchhiker was this couple's first, and they didn't know what they were doing. The mute connection between the girl and the wife could spur the wife to talk her husband into changing the plan. The husband could allow his wife to have this girl all to herself because the wife had taken a fancy. The wife could convince her husband that this girl was substandard, not worth the effort. The wife could refuse to participate. Something important in the husband's outer life could take him away on business, leaving the wife and the girl alone so they could establish the plan.

She would do two versions, one with the violence intact and one in which the captive, murderer's wife in tow, goes free.

The night after they returned from their Christmas in Kashag, Hank had to work. Peck brought Burt home from his walk then decided to go out again. She tramped snow chunks through the house. She wrapped plastic bags around both versions of her play and her model of the basement closet where the kidnapping couple stashed the girl hitchhiker. Burt followed, leather leash slapping furniture. She dumped kibble in his bowl and refreshed his water.

"Be a good boy."

Burt cocked an ear, and she headed back out, plastic bag in mittened hand.

Snow specks muted the lamplight. Beyond that, flakes ranging from spots to clumps floated against the sky's mauve sheen. Two shuffled lanes trailed behind her even though she lifted her feet high.

She didn't think about what she'd do when she got there. She hadn't worn a scarf or hat. The constant wet drop chilled her neck.

A string of blue lights trimmed Mona and Jim's roof. Through the vertical blinds a tree glowed blue.

She thumped up the steps and shook herself. She took her mittens off and flicked the snow from her hair. Her wet hands ached, the thin wool scant protection.

She rang the doorbell and resisted the urge to stamp her feet. She picked up the bag then set it down again. The inside lights were on. Classical music played. She waited longer than a person should wait when no one answered. She rang again, a double ring, the kind that annoyed. She lifted one foot then the other, put her mittens back on, and picked up the bag. She coughed and sniffed and pressed her swimming nostrils against her cuff. Then she knocked the brass lion head and added a few knuckle raps. Snow eddies muttered around her as first the porch then the hallway went dark. Someone on the other side watched her. She couldn't move now if she tried. Finally the lock creaked, the bolt thudded, and the door swung open. Beyond the porch, the snow swirled blue. She opened the screen door and entered. The blue tree twinkled.

A man said, "Close the door and lock it."

She hadn't seen Jim since the summer. The voice was deep but strangled, as if the speaker were gargling. She could open the door and slip back into the snow. But the voice expected obedience and obedience was easy to give.

He sat in shadow on the couch, one knee crossed over the other, a book open on his lap.

"An unexpected surprise," he said. "This wasn't part of the plan. Come in. Have a seat."

The silhouette was Jim's. Peck sat on the floor and placed the bag on the sparkly white tree skirt beside a few wrapped boxes.

"Is someone else here?"

"Do you see anybody else?"

"I thought I heard another man."

"You didn't."

"Is Mona here?"

Jim stayed silent and so did Peck.

Jim was playing a role. A quiet one that disliked interruptions and had to regroup when his plan veered off course. One that liked symphony orchestras not hair bands. Without the story, she didn't know what to do, what could happen. A random element in this scenario, she could script the scene through her actions. No harm would come to her beside the sterile Christmas tree with snow clusters swarming in the candy light. She'd spent many days in this room. It was Mona's place, and this was Mona's fiancé. Hartley Horse was a few streets away. Burt was waiting and Hank would come home soon.

Jim switched on a lamp. He looked himself.

He asked about her studies, her visit up north, Hank's job, her dog. Peck leaned back on her hands, elbows locked. In her relief, she chatted away. She mimicked the Sergeant and bragged about how she didn't need to study for Calculus. Jim smiled often.

Mona must be at her parents'. She didn't dare ask again. Maybe she should leave. Mona might think it weird if she found her there. Especially with Jim acting one of his serial killer roles. He must have snapped out of it. He said he had self-control. Didn't he wish he could give into the urge and be the real thing? Another question she was afraid to ask.

Jim got them each a glass of pop with ice. He talked about his holidays and his exams and how he used the Four Ds of Success: Drive, Dedication, Determination and Desire. He repeated the Four Ds.

"Remember them," he said. "They apply to everything. Exams, naturally, but to anything else in life you would ever want to do. Anything. You imagine it, you work it through in your mind, then you apply these Four Ds and you have your key to success."

He said them a third time and had her repeat after him.

"Do you still read true crime?" he asked.

"Always." She didn't tell him how guilty she'd felt reading it in recent months.

"Which ones?"

She recited titles of books about husband-and-wife teams who kept hitchhikers as slaves in cellars converted to dungeons.

"I've never practised a kidnapper," he said.

She chugged her pop. Ice cubes smashed her teeth. She told him how these crimes worked best with a pretty female accomplice, how a young hitchhiker never suspected a husband and wife of harm, especially if they had a baby, though a baby wasn't necessary. The wife didn't have to participate beyond that. Sometimes, though, the wife was as bad as her husband. Two people might kidnap a girl for various reasons. To keep her, maybe, or worse.

She lowered her head and said, "You know all this. You're an expert and I'm not telling you anything new."

"You are, believe it or not. You are giving me ideas."

"What, for different scenarios to act out? Different murders to try? Almost try?"

"Exactly that. I'll have to check out these stories you've been reading. I'm interested in where your head's at. You have an unusual mind for someone your age. Any age. But something more, too."

He shook his glass so the cubes clattered.

"I'm thinking about how to take a number of these stories,

the ones you've read recently. These are not household names. These guys didn't become famous for their crimes. Plus, there is a similarity in their actions. What if we create a composite, invent our own murderer to act out, make it new, not copied. The possibilities are endless. We figure it out beforehand so we know what our guy is capable of and where to stop."

"I did that."

His pupils shrank. "What?"

"What you said."

"You've thought about this?" His mouth slackened. "Tell me. I want to know about it." He rearranged his features into an expression of indulgence and delight that she didn't quite trust.

She revealed a bit about the plays she'd done with Mona, a betrayal if Mona hadn't told him. A betrayal even so. He urged her on. "Go, go."

She stuck to the version she'd designed to appeal to him.

"None of it is real. None of it happened that way."

"In a sense, it did, Peck, because you read the books, and they were true, and you thought about the crimes and you distilled them through your imagination to create this composite. So it did happen, all of it, at various hands, in various places. You've taken it and made it your own, made it real for us. It's brilliant. I want to see it. Do you have it?"

Peck took out the closet model. She turned the bag inside out, but the play in its two versions was not there.

She showed Jim the closet. The door on its mini swinging hinges, the carpet lining, and the scrap of brown sleeping bag, edges blanket-stitched in orange thread.

"Where's the script?" he asked, too soon.

She offered to run home and get it.

He wanted her to stay. He made her repeat the story and interrupted her with questions about action and location, "logistics," he said.

They spent a long time going through the story this way. Jim toyed with the model's tiny door, angled at the top to match the incline of the stairs it was tucked under.

"Would you do this? he asked. "Is this why you're telling me? This is something you want? You thought of it and wrote it up. You went to the trouble. The model is fair proof, so I have to trust that you didn't conveniently forget the script. The rest is hard to believe. Why would you want to?"

"The same reason you do."

He examined her.

"Come here. I have something to show you."

She scooped up the model and followed him down the hall. Her thumb closed the little hiding place door. Jim stood outside the spare room she'd stayed in the night of the sleepover, his hand on the wall.

When she stopped, Jim beckoned her closer. She took one step. He opened the door and switched on the light. On the bed sat Mona, straight-backed, arms behind her, chin high. Pantyhose stretched her mouth and the hair from a side-parted brown wig fell down her back. She wore a pink shorty bathrobe with a slip draped across her shoulders. Another pair of nylons hitched her ankles under the bed.

"A Boston Strangler victim."

Mona allowed fear to rinse her eyes when she looked at Jim. Then her lids dropped.

"Open," he whispered.

She obeyed, her eyes blank, yet lightly knowing.

He bent her torso forward to show Peck the nylons lashing her wrists. When he fixed Mona back in position, her robe flipped up, whether by accident or by his design, revealing a white wedge of panty.

Mona cast one more fake, scared look at Jim. He stepped into the hall, turned off the light, and closed the door. Peck wanted to go back in. She shouldn't believe the fear Mona switched on and off. It was part of the game. When she and Mona acted together, they became the characters. Mona and Jim must do the same thing. Only here, Mona had changed into someone Peck didn't want, a weak, wiped-clean Mona, her sham fear banal. Peck didn't like seeing Mona shape herself in such a vacuous way for Jim.

Outside the room, Jim's arm circled Peck's shoulder. He bent and found her with his hot, airless mouth. Her nails dug at his collarbone. Mona was acting a role with Jim and not her. She fixed Mona in her mind and bit into the kiss.

Afterward, in the living room, Jim brought up the play.

"You should be the accomplice. You're not underage, but it's tricky territory if you play the victim."

Behind that door, Mona had sat in the quickening air as the kiss took root. Jim's smile said what the kiss said, that we might start out one way but we can change and change and change, that the way we start out doesn't have to be the way we end up. Roles can switch, and rules can shift. It's all part of this game we're playing. If you're willing.

She was willing.

For the rest of the holidays, Peck took the play over to Jim and Mona's every day. She waited, but no one answered. It didn't snow again, so she couldn't check for footprints. They must have their lights on a timer.

When she was not walking Burt, she stayed in her room. She wrote the Four Ds of Success in calligraphy on a card she taped beside her John Lennon banner and Mona's typed-out "Rapunzel." She wanted to see Mona, had to see her. She imagined variations on kissing Jim, sitting on the couch, lying down in the car, that grappling kiss, and no more. She'd never fantasized about kissing Malcolm. In her scenarios, Mona watched while tied to a kitchen chair, or stalked in nude, narrow-eyed, nails scraping as she yanked Peck away from her fiancé.

A week after school started, she rang the doorbell at 17 Covered Wagon Trail, and Mona answered. Her hair hung to her shoulders, the ends and the bangs bleached white. She wore a white sleeveless turtleneck that ended under her boobs and had a circle cut out of the back with black stirrup pants and the gold ankle boots she called her Peter Pan getaway boots. Peck had on flowered acid-washed jeans Hank had given her for Christmas and one of his shirts with a brooch worn at the collar the way the girls at Western Secondary did.

They sat in the living room with tumblers of Tab and ice. Peck kept the bag with Mona's version of the play on her lap. Mona talked about the law school New Year's party and the Christmas gift Jim had given her, a matching gold chain, bracelet, and anklet set that said "Spoiled." She talked about registering for her wedding and how she couldn't wait to get married. Neither mentioned Mona and Jim acting out the Boston Strangler.

"I wrote a new one, the kind you wanted. I've got it here."

"I know."

"He told you?"

"He tells me everything. Don't worry. You can't have a secret about him from me."

Peck didn't dare mention the kiss.

"He told me what the play is about and it sounds like what we were looking for," Mona said, her tone secretarial.

"You have to read it. He didn't. I've got it here."

"It'll be different than what we've done before. I haven't told him how much I want you involved. He has to want it on his own, separately of me. He does, don't you think?"

"I guess so."

"So it's good, it's all good. We'll have to figure out a convenient time. He's in his final semester, but he should have time around Reading Week. You might have to take a day off school."

"Don't you want to read it?"

"I don't need to, do I? Jim told me the story so I know what happens. No offence, but knowing the script has never helped me before. Once I'm in it, I'm in it and it happens. The drag about February is the cold. You'll have to hitchhike in the snow."

"I will?"

"Did you think I would be playing the hitchhiker? No. That

role is so yours. There's no reason for me to play the victim. Not if we've got someone else."

"I thought you liked it," Peck said. Her mind flashed on a gagged, bewigged Mona knotted to a bed.

"I can do it, but it's me, no matter how much we pretend. It will go better with a new person, especially with a new story. You wouldn't believe how impressed he is with you, he keeps telling me."

Peck detected some jealousy. Mostly she heard eagerness.

"Don't worry about your age. You're legal. Besides, if it was going to be a problem it would be a problem no matter which role you played. Nothing will happen that you can't handle."

Peck tried to convince Mona to read her script again, but she refused. Finally she told her about the version where the victim and the wife form an alliance and both go free.

"Why would the wife want to go free? She's with her husband. That's her life."

"Because of that life. She's only doing whatever he wants because she loves him."

"How do you know that? How do you know she doesn't want to on her own?" Mona set her glass on a cork coaster.

"Why would she want to commit his crimes? To kidnap, rape, and torture his victims? To kill?"

"You are missing a fine distinction here, darling. It is not that she wants to do these things you mention, to rape, torture, and kill. She is not a rapist. She is no sadist, nor a murderer. And it's not that she wants to do these things *because* he wants her to. She wants to do these things *with him*. That's the point. To explore with him the things he wants to do and to find ways to make them possible. That is why your play wouldn't work the way you've written it. The wife stays. She wants to."

"But she could be free."

"She is free."

chapter 11

Look at me now, I wanted to say to Joy in her front-row seat. Look at me, a shadowy, beautiful woman, telling my story with passion and dignity, sexy, dangerous, everything I liked to believe Ramona thought about me. Here I am, the witness who reluctantly reveals her part in the sordid past of the accused, the witness whose fragile strength inspires forgiveness, wonder, even love. Facing down my tormentor, damaged but clear, my role defined, my story heroic.

The real me was anything but. In Joy's sketches, my pie-face had few lines and old, alien eyes. "I'm not very good," she'd said yesterday, when she showed me how she'd drawn me on the stand, but she was too good, really. Cindy had nailed me when she said "a doll on a shelf." Each word tired me out, and I slouched, my feelings messy, unable to focus and take aim at the enemy. My voice flat, I got asked to speak up, repeat. I delivered my story automatically, a robot witness, programmed by lawyers and cops. Nothing special or risky about me. Duller than the others. Barely there.

"Can you identify the woman in Exhibit Eighty-One?" Ron asked. He wore the same suit as the day before. Same shirt, for all I could tell.

"Yes," I said. "That's Ramona." Since I'd seen her photos at the police interview, I expected this part to be easier than the rest of the testimony. It was, if I didn't look too closely.

"How about Eighty-Two?"

"Ramona."

"Eighty-Three? Eighty-Four? Eighty-Five?"

"All Ramona."

"How do you know, specifically?"

"I don't know." I had lost my head for details.

"When did you see the witness's body without clothing?"

"I saw her while she was changing. I never saw her naked in that way." I remembered Lyndsey Franklin avoiding looking at Ramona. With me it was worse. My gaze skipped over Ramona as if the space she occupied didn't exist. I didn't look at Ron either, or the judge, or my dad. If I scanned the room without cease, I could make the experience feel like a dream.

"What do you mean by 'in that way'?" Ron asked.

"Sexually. I never saw her naked in a sexual way." Since Ramona, I'd hated saying the words for body parts or sex acts out loud. Answering Ron's questions had a doctor's office quality, though. My actions became clinical and the words lost their weight. I could say "sexual" now and it had nothing to do with sex. More importantly, it had nothing to do with me and sex.

"What did you observe about the skin of the accused when you saw her changing clothes?"

"I don't remember." Stick to the facts, Ron had said before the trial. Don't say anything you don't believe to be true.

"It was summer when you knew her. What sort of clothing did the accused wear?"

"Tank tops, shorts. We both did."

"What did her skin look like?"

"Normal. Smooth and tanned."

"I'd like you to take a look at Exhibit Eighty-Six. Do you recognize this one?"

"That's me."

"I don't have to ask how you know that, but I will ask you this: what do you remember about having this picture taken?"

"Nothing."

Bill Witherson stood, dropping papers. "Objection," he said. "Your Honour, if she doesn't remember having it taken, she is hardly in a position to state when it was taken."

"Your Honour, if I may, there are other clues that the witness may be able to respond to that will enable her to situate the photograph in time, which will be helpful to the court in light of her involvement with the accused and her husband."

The judge spoke. "The evidence is relevant. I will admit it. Proceed."

"Ms. Brown, when was this photograph taken?"

"It was the night I stayed over to help Ramona plan her engagement party, the night I fell asleep on the floor."

"How do you know?"

"Partly because of the brown and yellow afghan but also because of the 1/2 Moon wrapper in the corner. The freckles on my chest and shoulders mean the photo was taken in the summer. I used to wear tank tops with spaghetti straps. That was the only night I ever stayed over and I ate three 1/2 Moons." Actually I prefer Sno Balls, I wanted to say, though the joke was too lame to cheer me up.

"Can you tell the court exactly what night it was?"

"I know it was a Tuesday, because Wednesdays were my days off from Venus Video. End of August. I don't remember the date."

"Thank you, Ms. Brown. There's one more, if you wouldn't

mind. Your Honour, I'd like permission to enter this photograph as evidence.

I had seen the Polaroid Ron was about to lay on me. There was only one of its kind. Though I didn't expect to see it blown up to poster size and mounted on a cardboard stand.

The photograph shows Ramona close up, in a ski jacket, eyes half shut and satisfied. Her cheek against a pigeon-like breast, bent tongue tip on a rounded nipple. One elbow points up and her fisted fingers yank the pubic curls taut. Lines fan the corded thigh where her thumb digs deep. The other woman's raised arms block her face except for her square chin. Coal freckles dust her waxen chest.

On its own, the photograph proved nothing. It was hard to tell if the woman was willing, or even conscious. Ron placed the poster at an angle for the jury then stuck the original near my face and wouldn't let up until I told him more.

As I spoke, a lightness overtook me. Talking about my naked body to the detectives had been bizarre enough. In the smoky room, my words had shimmered like a secret the detectives would protect. Now the lawyer had me on surreal display, both on the stand and in this poster of a naked teenager too stoned and foolish to know what was happening to her.

The back door opened and my dad slipped out. Or maybe a vision of my dad, I couldn't tell. I half-stood. I wanted out of the witness box, out of the courtroom. Here I was, about to tell the most crucial part, and he was leaving. Maybe he found my story dirty, degrading. At my convocation he'd told me he'd never gone to a lawyer over my mother, not because he pined for her but because he wanted me more, and if he took her back he could draw me home. "Nobody loves you like I do," he'd told me. Teary from his raw, abrasive need, I'd said "Thank you" and let him treat me to a pasta dinner while Alex took pictures on his Instamatic. Every weekend I meant to call him but I never had.

And Alex, where was he? I needed him here more. Even Ramona's family had come. None had ducked out. I bet she had a boyfriend stashed in the crowd, too. Or a girlfriend. I wanted to throw up. I wished I would. As each piece of this story came out, I felt more and more hollow. Soon I would have nothing left.

chapter 12

Peck's throat was dry. Wet cotton gripped her armpits. Her pantyhose crept south.

She'd done everything according to plan, but she didn't feel the same as she had alone with Mona. The role didn't take her over. She was herself in the middle of the scene.

The morning of the second Saturday in February, 1986, Peck stood on the highway wearing a white blouse with a baby blue Peter Pan collar; a baby blue cardigan; and a baby blue and brown plaid skirt, pleated like a kilt and falling above her knees. Mona's clothes. Thicker than Mona, she couldn't zip the skirt or button the blouse cuffs. Jim had wanted the look of a school uniform, so she'd agreed to this outfit. Over top, she wore Jim's old shearling car coat. Her hand hung slack, thumb hooked out. Cars splashed brown slushclots. No one stopped, 'thank God, until the couple pulled up in the maroon Escort. She hesitated, then got in. In the fairy tale plays, she'd had a delicious submersion in a part. Mona, too, had physically changed. Here,

Mona and Jim had transformed not into other characters, but into hard, ugly, meaner aspects of themselves. Peck stayed the same through all of it. Mona and Jim were sticking to her play with an accuracy that chilled Peck because it wasn't her story now. It was theirs. A cylinder nosed her back. Hands shackled her and held her under blankets. They'd forgotten the duct tape. At the first glimpse of her captors' cold eyes, she thought, *I'll submit to all of it and it'll go okay and they'll be nice to me.* When she did, they pushed her around more. They wanted struggle. So she fought.

They drove for a long time, turning left then right, east, west. She felt lost though she knew their destination. At Covered Wagon Trail, they walked her into the house with her head under the blanket. Inside they led her down a hall and into the basement.

Mona and Jim removed the blanket together. Their actions differed now from her play. Peck blinked in the dim light. Mona held a small gun. She had eyes as dull as the night Peck saw her tied to the waterbed, with the same inner knowing. She could be holding a starter pistol. Or a cap gun. She could be playing a game. Even if she tossed the pistol behind her, Peck would do what she asked. She wanted to please. They held their bodies tense, as if they expected resistance. A normal girl's reaction.

Jim opened a door. He'd cleaned out a crawl space and glued carpet strips onto the bluish grey floor and walls. Like Peck's model. Mona set the gun on a workbench and patted her jeans pockets. Peck lunged clumsily. Both were on her in an instant. All three fell to the floor. Jim's and Mona's full weights dropped into her and she went limp. Then they released her. Mona rested the gun against Peck's shoulder.

"What do you want?" Peck asked.

"You'll see."

Jim drew his lips back from his teeth and kissed her. Rough bones and dry skin. The tongue wormed around her gums, tasting of bleach. It was nothing wonderful. Mona nudged her face in, too. Peck gagged. Then, as Mona licked and nipped and sucked her cringing tongue forward, she found herself gobbling at Mona's apple-sweet mouth, her own breath stopped high in her chest, thighs aching twists. Mona pushed her.

"This is what it's going to be, and you can cooperate or not. Nothing's going to change. We'll keep you in the closet when we're not using you."

Peck scuttled back on her haunches until her spine hit concrete, one shoulder under the workbench. Jim kneeled. He winked at Mona, who crawled up to Peck. No one moved. No one talked. Her breathing slowed.

Mona's taste lingered, and her slipperiness. Peck resisted the urge to lick her lips. Mona gripped her chin and straightened her face. She inched forward until their noses touched.

"I won't need the cuffs."

Jim crept upstairs. Peck got lost in the asphalt eyes, the tarry pupils. No matter how far they had strayed from each other, Mona had surprised her before by reminding her of who they were.

"That kiss," Mona said.

"I liked it," Peck said. "With you."

Mona interrupted. "Did you see her? Me? California trailer trash hooked up with a dangerous badass, someone who'll make me do things I never dreamed of. I became her, didn't I? And you. You turned into the scared little schoolgirl. It's the same as when you became the witch and I was Rapunzel. Only now I'm the kidnapper and you're the victim."

"Yes, yes," Peck said. She drew her face closer. She would say anything now.

"And Jim is part of it. You understand. You feel it."

Her fingers were cold. She'd like to tap Mona's skin and watch her jump. Dig into Jim's windpipe. A speedy TV voice came from above. She wouldn't admit that she hadn't seen the blonde trailer trash or turned into the frightened schoolgirl, but she hadn't. With Jim there, she'd stayed herself through all of it.

"I can do it, but I'm me no matter how much we pretend," Mona had said about playing roles with Jim. Mona hadn't become the character with Jim until Peck joined in. She needed Peck to make that change happen.

Mona shifted her blank stare to a full-on warmth that encircled Peck. A lover's gaze. A mother's. The craved connection. She'd hold on to this look when Jim came back and Mona switched off her affection.

Mona stroked her hand and moved closer, like the princess and the crone and their arm-against-arm discoveries. Mona showed how she felt, didn't say. Peck would act with them because Mona wanted it. She would give Mona anything. She had betrayed her by kissing her fiancé. Not now, as part of their game, but with Mona tied up inside the guest room. She shouldn't have kissed Jim then. It didn't matter how mad she'd been or that she'd thought of Mona the whole time. To make up for that kiss, she would surrender now and devote herself to Mona.

Jim came down with a glass of wine. Mona stood before he reached the bottom.

"Get up," he said.

She did, her back flat against the rough wall. Her palms brushed the skirt's acrylic pleats.

He handed the glass to Mona, who passed it to Peck. She drank it right down, eyes lowered. Mona lifted Peck's left leg from behind its knee and rolled down the pantyhose. Jim breathed wetly by the stairs. Mona stretched the pantyhose off her feet, took the wineglass and placed it on the workbench. She pulled her away from the wall then eased the sweater sleeves off. Peck shut her eyes and imagined Mona hooking her into the corset. Only Mona existed for Peck. No blonde California badass. No trailer trash. Together, though, Jim and Mona kept up the act.

Mona unbuttoned her blouse and cuffs and unzipped the kilt. The clothes dropped. Mona heaped the clothes on the workbench.

There was a flash and a grind-click as Jim snapped a Polaroid. Peck burned at how she must look in Mona's white push-up bra and flowered granny panties, the kind Jim said a schoolgirl wore. She hadn't checked in a mirror earlier and had tried not to think about Jim seeing her as she got dressed. He and Mona could look back at these photos and remember. They might even show other people. Peck dug her nails into her palms. She wanted to cross her legs and cover her chest but worried she'd make a wrong move.

Everything flowed in slow motion. Peck's skin tingled. Her mouth felt gooey. Jim dashed up the stairs two at a time and returned with another glass of wine.

"Drink," he said. He didn't touch her, only looked and raised the camera. She hunched her shoulders. He waved the pictures in arcs and figure eights as shapes emerged.

Mona brushed off sawdust then patted the workbench. Peck got on her back, knees raised, Mona's hands on her hips. Jim said, "Fuck this. Stop. This isn't right."

He chucked the camera. It landed on her clothes.

"This is too easy. This is not what I wanted. It's not the way it should be, the way it *would* be. She is doing everything you want."

"She wants it as badly as we do, Jim. Look at her there, waiting to do whatever we tell her. I could slip off her panties, open her up, and put my face there while you took pictures, and she would let me. She wants me. She wants you, too."

"She wants me what?"

"You know."

"Say it, bitch."

"To fuck her, okay? Because she thinks that's what I want. What she wants is for *me* to fuck her. She wants it in her pathetic little way because she thinks she's in love with me. She thinks she's better than you and that she and I are meant to be together, but we aren't. She doesn't want to do this. She's pretending. But she doesn't know we're serious. That it was all a con. She's got her own con going on."

Tools swam beyond their pegboard outlines as Peck struggled up. Mona had it wrong. She didn't think she was in love.

She was. Mona's hands stilled her hips. Only someone who knew her feelings could slant them so well.

She propped herself on her elbows and Mona forced her down, her eyes hateful now, beyond angry. She wore her ice pink ski jacket. She'd buzzed and bleached her hair like Wendy O. Williams, only cuter. Jim's hair curled over his plaid collar. When he became a lawyer, he'd wear a gown and a fussy white collar. The Peter Pan collar had choked Peck. Peter Pan never wore a Peter Pan collar. He wore a green tunic. Or was that Robin Hood? Did he wear Peter Pan getaway boots? Peck's eyelids dropped, fluttered, then shut. When she moved an arm or a leg, she felt a delay, like the air was holding her in place.

Rough hands pulled her underwear then her breasts. Resistance surged. Girls in her position rebelled, so she would, too. If she acted her part, maybe the schoolgirl kidnap victim would take her over the way the witch had. She tried jabbing her elbows and kicking but ended up flinging her limbs. Mona's mouth clamped on hers, and Jim's hand over her eyes crushed her temples. Her legs were wrenched apart and damp air hit. Mona's thumb caught skin as she pushed it in then jerked it out, and it hurt.

"Look," Mona said. Jim took his hand away and pulled Peck's head up by the hair. Mona held her thumb toward him as if she were displaying a contact lens. She traced a warm, wet trail on Peck's thigh and said, "Told you she wants it."

Mona licked her thumb then jacked more fingers up and down in slippery circles. Peck rolled her eyes back and tried to close her thighs against her wetness, her urge to clench Mona's hand. Her skin felt torn. It pricked and itched like nettle stings, smarted like paper cuts. Mona shouldered her leg wide, dragged her fingers out, then slammed knuckles. Peck's bones throbbed, lips sticky and sore. Pain stitched her nipples. Mona drove doubled fingers, corkscrewed knuckles, opened and rocked her hand forward. She drew her arm back and, in one long, unbroken thrust, forced what felt like her whole hand inside. Peck's entire body shot into motion. She wasn't acting now. She bucked her hips and shoulders and screamed into Mona's gulping mouth until Mona ripped her hand away and smacked a slick fist against Peck's thigh. Peck's knees flew up, and her arms jolted as she curled against the shredded cut feeling. Then metal circled her wrists and and a crackly tape strip flattened her lips together. Pain billowed as arms lifted her through the shadow-edged air, laid her on the mouldy carpet, and closed the closet door. She couldn't raise her head. After a long unconsciousness, she awoke humming against the tape. Still, she questioned her role. Did they want her to scream? Was screaming part of the kidnap victim's character? Her tailbone ached. Warm liquid coated her legs. The carpet squeaked wet and cool. Then what was already black and already silent receded and she was gone.

She was taken out once, maybe twice, laid on the workbench, on her stomach, her back. Mona's mouth travelled her skin, and her fingers mashed inside her, sometimes with a cold jelly squeezed from a metal tube. She didn't feel much. Each time they took her out, she had more to drink. She remembered little except popping flashes and Mona's hands. Jim must have fixed the camera. Sometimes she torqued herself and kicked, but her actions made no difference. This was what they were doing. This was who they were to each other now.

Mona said things like, "You know you want us — you always wanted us — that's why you kept hanging around."

She called Peck "slut" and "bitch" and "whore."

"You want to fuck my fiancé? Sorry, cunt. You got me instead," Mona said and rammed her hand.

Peck rode the pain. Her punishment. Mona was wrong about Peck wanting her fiancé. The kiss was a betrayal based never in desire, only opportunity. Afterwards, Mona's reaction had dominated any scenarios Peck imagined with Jim. Mona, she'd wanted, more than anyone.

She gave up on Mona and sought Jim's eyes instead. Other than covering her eyes and yanking her hair, he hadn't touched her. Peck couldn't fix him in her sights. He crouched in corners and snapped photos. Mona's mouth between her legs, Mona's cheek on her breast.

chapter 13

The clock read ten minutes to four as I ended my story on Thursday, April 23. Ron lobbed more questions, but I remembered less and less. I didn't know how long I'd stayed in the closet under the basement stairs. I'd fallen asleep and woken up there. I didn't know if something in the wine had made me tired. I'd heard the phone. No, they'd never hit me. They'd never slapped me. They'd done nothing rough with me other than wrestle me to the ground when I'd lunged and, of course, the sex. Yes, they'd kissed me, they'd both kissed me, separately and at the same time. I didn't remember if James Hawkes had had sex with me. I thought he hadn't. I didn't remember going home.

Excerpt from Transcript
RAMONA HAWKES
v
HER MAJESTY THE QUEEN

————

April 23, 1992
Toronto, Ontario

————

MR. LAURIE:	Try to remember. Are you sure nothing else happened?
MS. BROWN:	I don't remember. Ramona let me out, and I came upstairs to her bedroom and changed.
MR. LAURIE:	Where was James?
MS. BROWN:	I don't know.
MR. LAURIE:	Where was Ramona?
MS. BROWN:	She stayed with me, but she didn't watch me. We talked. Like normal. She said my father called.
MR. LAURIE:	What happened after that?
MS. BROWN:	Nothing.
MR. LAURIE:	How many times did you see James Hawkes after that?
MS. BROWN:	None. I never saw him again.
MR. LAURIE:	And Ramona? How many times did you see her again?
MS. BROWN:	I didn't see her again either. I graduated from high school and left for university not long after that. I didn't even go to their wedding. Our friendship was over.
MR. LAURIE:	Did anything else happen?
MS. BROWN:	No. Nothing.

At the end of my second day of testimony at the Ramona Hawkes trial, I was standing at the back door with a court officer when the registrar called, "Order in the court. All rise! I declare this court adjourned." Everyone in the courtroom paused, wavering, until Ramona Hawkes gripped the table, her wrists linked, and pushed herself to her feet. She moved like a heavy or a fatigued woman, a woman with no will. I dismissed the possibility of suicide. I doubted she'd have the energy.

The moment passed cleanly and forgettably. Soon Justice Larraby had gone and two court officers in Kevlar vests escorted Ramona out the side. The lawyers followed. I left through the wooden double doors and rounded the corner before people from the gallery filed out.

My chest stretched. I had said it. All the truth I could muster. My lungs heaved, but my breath stayed measured, hibernation slow.

What happened with Ramona and James had the quality of events in a book or a movie rather than life. Yet the experience felt more mine than ever.

Voices echoed up the escalators. Bodies jostled past. Cindy zoomed toward me from one direction. Joy signalled from another. Guards whisked Ramona into the elevator. I stared, ready for her now, but she didn't look.

Cindy reached me first. I had no problem meeting her eyes. I smiled. When she invited me to a summit over dinner, no obligation, I bobbed my head as if I were listening to a Walkman. Cindy could turn me into a cartoon character for all I cared. Nothing could change the details now. My words cemented them.

I'd given the Crown everything he wanted.

I'd played the surprise witness well.

The hall emptied out. A few people waited at the elevator. Three lawyers cackled by the double doors of Courtroom 7-2. I saluted Joy and left Cindy with a mild wave.

Everybody knew my appetite for pain now. For years, I'd kept Ramona in a barren place and let shame corrode any feeling. I'd labelled it friendship, ventured to call it love, but it wasn't like the love I had with Alex. I had wanted Ramona, even when she was rough, abusive, cold — especially then — but Ramona had hinged that lust on James and exposed me. Could she have desired me, too, despite her meanness, or as part of it? I wanted to understand.

I took the stairs and exited onto University. An ascending rib cage of lights blinked against fat denim clouds atop the Canada Life building. A cold wind shot around my neck and skimmed my forehead as I crossed University. I fastened my trench coat and headed for St. Mary's Hospital. I passed under the swooping concrete awning and through the sliding doors into Emergency.

A man holding his palm over his eye stood in front of a glassed-off room. A nurse in a pink top and pants spoke to him through a microphone. He responded into a circular steel vent built into the glass.

Through a slot, the nurse passed him a clipboard with a pen attached by a silver-balled chain and instructed him to come back when he had filled out the form. When I stepped up, the nurse asked for my health card. I kept my head down. Though papers hadn't printed my picture — they hadn't shown any of Ramona's former friends — I worried that the nurse might recognize me.

"I'd like to see my husband," I said. Again, the word sounded odd. Foreign. "He's one of the interns."

"Who is he?" The nurse had glossy black hair, curled in rolls at the sides.

"Alexander Shore."

"Spell it?"

"S - H - O - R- E."

"Okay. It sounded like you said *Shaw*." The nurse checked a clipboard chart hooked on the wall. The phone rang, and she picked it up and said, "Emerge." She listened, pushed a button, and hung up.

"His name has been scratched off."

"Is there anyone I can talk to? I need to see him."

"You can wait for one of the doctors, dear, but they're busy.

If he's not here, he's not here."

"It doesn't look busy." In the waiting area, the man balanced his clipboard on his knee while trying to cup his eye and fill in the form at the same time.

The nurse stared. Her hair rolls drooped forlornly. Then she picked up the phone and turned her back to me.

I sat in an orange plastic chair. On a TV near the ceiling, a couple on a floral couch talked about the glory of abstaining from sex until marriage. The number for a prayer hotline wound past. The nurse came back. When I stood, she showed me her palm and gave her head one shake. I sat.

When I'd left Alex without saying goodbye or doing any of our morning rituals, I'd felt strong and rebellious. He couldn't face my pleasure, or his own. I'd used my time at the Buttercup to write. Now, my story out, I regretted not having left him a note telling him where I was going and why.

I jumped up with my thumb and pinkie against my tilted head to mime a phone. The nurse pointed left and I strode down the hall. My finger poised to hang up, I called home. Alex's fake British accent announced his regrets that he and "the old trouble and strife" were indisposed. When he signed off with "Tally ho!" I held my breath. The machine beeped once. Last night I'd counted four, one per message. I hung up. He'd come home.

I leaned my forehead on the black box. *I left him.* The words clanged through me with each footfall as I headed back onto the street.

I passed a tented hot dog cart then headed east under a bridge and around a copper-roofed clock tower until I stood under three arches at Nathan Philips Square. I wasn't ready to go home yet. The city had drained the ice but hadn't turned on the fountain. I took a bench near the edge. My skort rode up my thighs. In July, the sun allowed little shade this time of day and the tops of buildings cut the sky, the bench hot enough to brand skin. Not like the April mute of grey on grey offered now, the bench so cold my legs felt wet.

Maybe I hadn't consented to Ramona's fingers and sickening language after all. Ramona had tricked, drugged, seduced, and ignored me. But *I* had written the play. I had added what James liked, and I had dressed up and acted out the role. I didn't say "Yes," but I could have said "Stop." I could have said "This hurts." I could have said many things, but I didn't. Ramona opened my legs and sank her fingers and I didn't say "No" to what I should have refused.

I had resisted the telling. I had liked having control of my story, though the secret had denied anger and fed shame. If I told, my dad might call me a disappointment. Jenna would look at me as if I were a freak and say I'd let two people take advantage of me. Alex would say, "So what? You did something kinky."

A woman in a dirty beige sweater-coat sat down on the next bench and murmured a song to a white dog wrapped in a red scarf. She called the dog Suicide, her voice a caress. The dog pawed the air like a hamster on a wheel. I got up and walked into the middle of the square and looked straight up at what seemed less a sky than a low grey cap on things, a formless wrapper that sealed us all here together, me and Ramona and the woman and Suicide. Such a sign meant I should get far away from the woman with the white dog, but then I guessed she'd chosen Suicide as a means of explaining herself up front, and that maybe she had the right idea.

I circled behind City Hall and came out north of 361 University. The concourse in front of the courthouse was deserted. A Barbie bride and Ken groom covered in red paint hung from a tree. Down the street, Alex leaned against Osgoode's metal fence.

Alex wore a peacoat and red basketball shoes. Frizzled tabs of hair escaped like pinfeathers from his ball cap. His shoulders hunched near his ears, and he caught each breath for a still moment. Anger flattened his eyes, along with a feral sadness. I stood a few feet away, my trench coat open.

"You didn't have to —" I said. My voice came out fainter than I intended, the honeyed tone I used on him to get agreement, a smile. My body felt slimy, swollen. I didn't want him to touch me.

"No, you're right." He kept his hands in his pockets. I shrank, a hurt, wet lump. The disgrace I'd always felt I deserved.

"I looked for you at the trial, and after I finished I went over to the hospital. They couldn't find you. They said you didn't go in yesterday, either."

"How could I? My wife left me." The skin around his eyes reddened, wrinkle-cracked like desert clay. He had the air of another man, an inconsolable man — one I'd never loved — whose wife had abandoned him. I was that wife, and I had made him feel that way.

He blinked, and his eyelashes clotted. He shook his hand free of his pocket and gave me a humid look. He gripped my wrist.

"Don't do it again," he said. I couldn't tell if he was serious.

"You don't usually follow the news."

"I did read. And I listened. But it wasn't hard to find you. We talked about it — remember?" Lips rolled back, he pissed his words out. His bottom teeth overlapped, a detail I hadn't noticed before.

I wanted to rush past this part, into an embrace, home to some forgiving sex, a good cry, then move on. I might settle for a return to our silent rhythm before I found out about James's death if it meant an end to facing the suffering my life caused in Alex. I dropped his hand.

"There's more I want to tell you. Or show you. I've been writing it down, a few pieces here, a few pieces there. What I said on the stand along with details about my family and where I lived. I could write the rest for you. It might help make things right between us."

His face puckered and he looked to the side, blinking. "I know what they did to you," he said. "I don't need more details."

"You don't know what I said today. And the papers won't get it right. You should have come. We didn't plan for it, but you should have. Even my dad came today."

"So did I." He spread his hands, palms up.

"To the trial?" I had not wanted Alex there. Though he'd suggested it, I'd insisted on going alone. He didn't remind me now.

"I came after lunch."

"I didn't see you."

"I guess I made a real impression. But you saw your dad."

"I saw him leave. He scooted out after the photograph so he missed the best part." My sarcasm fizzled. Alex sniffed.

"Alex, thank you, thank you for coming."

"It wasn't the easiest thing I've done." He rocked back on his heels, his smile a feint.

"But, Alex, I do need you to know what happened, to understand how it connects to us."

"Don't tell me you did these things while we were together, Pauline." His face tensed.

"No, not that. Other things."

"So you lied on the stand? You said nothing else happened. Why would you?"

"I didn't lie. I told them what happened, what they asked. The rest had nothing to do with Ramona."

"That's for the lawyers to decide."

"I need to tell you so you can see, as I said on the stand, that I agreed to do what I did."

"I don't believe that. And that's not what I heard you say. Even if you involved yourself in questionable events — don't you see they were predators?"

"I didn't then, but I do now. Even so, I helped set it up. My body responded to her. I'm not blameless."

"Those were extreme circumstances. You can't read any meaning into how your body reacts to undue stress."

"Nobody else has felt what I did."

"Nobody else has admitted it."

In true crimes, it was easy to see a killer's roots in the mother who locked him in a closet and gave him lemonade enemas. Easy, too, to forgive a victim who gives a kidnapper directions or, like the girl who inspired "Polly," pretends to enjoy the rape so she can go free. But what about those who fall under a killer's sway? The lovers who join the killers on crime sprees. The friends who play along with the games. Did a friend who asked Ramona Hawkes to do what she wanted — even if she later decided she'd had enough — really deserve what she got when Ramona went too far?

I relented. "Ramona did manipulate me, you could read it that way. But you could also see what happened as an education, or an initiation."

"Or a corruption."

"Or all of the above."

"She's manipulating you still if you see it any other way."

"You must have sensed you didn't know all of me." Unable to stop myself, I trotted out the old hurt. "You found somebody else."

"That's over," Alex said, "and it's not what we're talking about."

"Sure it is. We're saying everything now."

"What about you, then? You loved someone else all along. If we're saying everything, why aren't we saying how we feel?"

"We can. We should." Staring, I waited for him to speak first. He stared back, but neither of us would say "I love you," our standoff the best evidence that we still did.

Bending my arm behind my back, he pulled me to him, but I couldn't release into his hug. We stayed that way against the bars. Alex had fixed me in place as if he couldn't see past what happened with Ramona and James. He didn't get it. Testifying had unstitched me.

As he stroked my hair back, his thumb dusted my temple and I remembered the cut.

"I'm not like them," he said.

"It's okay whatever you're like."

"I didn't want to hurt you, Pauline."

"You wanted to please me, though, right?" I remembered his stony arousal when I handed him the knife.

"Maybe."

"It was good of you to give me what I wanted. You could do it again, and it would be okay. We might even."

"Would it mean you wouldn't leave?"

I struggled away from him, my head swaying, a child in the moment annoyed at him for getting to say the words I thought I owned. "What can I say to that?"

"Say you won't leave."

"I won't." For days, leaving Alex had distracted me, the wrongness of it and the choice. Now, my story out, Alex's sorrow irked me. My comfort should concern him most. Yet here was I, consoling him.

"You won't leave or you won't say it — which is it?"

"I'm sorry. I should have called when I stayed down here. Obviously I got scared. But I've had this big event in my life — my testimony's not over, even. Tomorrow's the cross. The hardest part. All you can think about are your own problems. You came today. You heard. Don't you think I might have more on my mind?" I kept my voice low and my eyes on his. People looked over their shoulders as they passed us. My part in Ramona's scene melted away. What had happened to me should disturb Alex. I wanted his outrage. His pity, too. It galled me that I did.

He fumed at me, red and silent.

"Say something." A sense of exile sank over me.

"You never get it, do you?"

"I guess I don't."

"I don't care what happened to you. I don't mean that like it sounds. I want you, what we have. I didn't know any of this before. It's a lot to digest."

"You're telling me. Imagine living it."

"But you said —"

"No matter what I did, you should want to make me feel better. And all you can think about is that I left you. For one night!"

164

"It's not how long you — it's that — I can see this trial is hard on you."

"Hard on me?" My skin tingled, and I let my voice out. "I wanted some connection from you."

"No. You wanted my attention."

"Your attention then. Fine. That night, the night before last. Maybe I went about it in a weird way. Maybe I couldn't handle it. But you don't get me. And you don't even try."

"I don't need to try. I know how I feel about you. You haven't let me inside since I've known you and now everything's out. It's natural to react."

"Hey, let me decide what's natural for me or not."

"Fine. Listen, though. Here we are in the middle of the street having a domestic. We can have a better argument in the car, no? Or at home. At least there, we'd have refreshments."

I liked the street. It kept me from crying. I didn't want to leave the courthouse, or the city even. If I did, I might not come back. I might skip the cross, risk contempt, have my story thrown out — not an unappealing idea. A story like mine deserved the trash.

Alex slipped on his British accent, in charm mode now. "We'll drive home together. Tomorrow I'll bring you in, sit in the front row. I should have come with you, you're right. I didn't know it until I saw you today. I'm a chickenshit."

"Alex, I've had enough of it."

"Of me?"

"Everything. I want you to go, leave me here. The trial is too much. It's all I can do."

"Wouldn't you feel better in your own bed?"

"Our bed makes me sad now. I don't trust myself there."

"What will you do? You don't know anybody. You haven't even told me where you're staying."

He looked past me, up the street to the hospital where he'd parked his car. When I didn't answer, he shrugged and walked north. He crossed in front of a surge of cars. His coat flapped. He didn't look back. Tired, I watched him go.

In our first semester at university, Jenna and I had gone to Montreal for a weekend and mistakenly taken a room on St. Catherine at a hotel that rented to hookers by the hour. The room smelled of stopped-up toilet and bleach. We watched the hookers from the window and concocted alternate lives for ourselves in the sex trade. Strippers. Phone sex workers. Dominatrices. Jenna thought she could. I said I could, too, but I was lying. Sex work felt too public and too personal. Too random. We split a mickey of vodka and went to a strip club where the men took everything off except their cowboy boots and the pop cost the same as the booze. I woke up in the sunlight to Jenna closing the door in her tennis shoes and jeans, her raw honey hair in chunky waves against her face. She'd gone out at 5:00 a.m., she reported, and taken two of the hookers for coffee. "One studies art, like you," she said.

I could stay in Toronto. I could go home. I didn't want either, but what was the alternative? The courthouse? Instead, I decided to drive awhile, see where I ended up. As I stood at the lights, a hand gripped my arm. Electric love and fear scorched my mind as I turned, my face crusted into a smile, for Alex. It was Joy.

The light changed, and we moved onto the street with the crowd. I caught the longing in her glare.

"What's wrong?" I asked.

"I was going to ask you the same thing."

"About me? I'm happy. I've told the story. All that's left is the cross and Ron told me what to expect. You're the one who seems pissed. What is it?"

"There's more. More than you said. I can tell." She stopped, one foot tucked around the back of her knee. "Withholding is lying, you know."

"I told them what they needed, what they asked me to tell." I entered the garage. I spotted the Hustler by the far wall.

"So there is more."

"There's always more."

"Will you tell me?"

We reached the truck. I unlocked both doors and got in. Joy stood hunched beside a concrete post. I saw what was familiar in her now and what was strange. Her hair held masses of light, like Jenna's did, and her eyes were the same pewter as Alex's and Mona's. Wide open, too, but not burning and not blank. Artless. I liked the blend.

"Wanna go for a ride?"

Joy wove through the crowd on Queen Street, hands in her vest pockets, not touching anyone. Fast. I took out my notebook and idled the truck while I waited for her to buy gum. Ramona could only have found out I'd kissed James if he'd told her. Or if he'd told someone else who'd then told her. Which he might have. To wound her.

Like James, I wanted to hurt her too, expose her to the core as she had done to me.

I picked up my story near the end — when I opened my eyes that afternoon in the basement workshop at 17 Covered Wagon Trail — and I made it about Pauline and Ramona. I left Peck and Mona out of it. I didn't need them now.

A block away, Joy was heading for the truck when I looked up, finished. I stuffed the notebook in my purse for later.

Cars lined the Gardiner ramp so I took Lakeshore Boulevard and ended up in another jam. At Parkside, I made a U-turn then got into the slow lane, going east. The lot beside the Lakeshore Canoe Club was deserted except for a boat trailer and a yellow camper van parked near the chain-link fence. A khaki green guardrail blocked the shore. I parked my truck at the opposite end from the van. I killed the engine. Bare-branched trees reached up from the lake stretched smooth as fresh-poured cement past the two-toned breakwater. Low navy clouds churned.

"Why don't we go hang out at the Buttercup," Joy said. She had full lips that narrowed to points. She probably had a great smile. I slipped my pumps off and drew one knee to my chest. Smudges greased the wet toes of my tights.

I slid the back window open. White noise from Lakeshore Boulevard swept the cab. Joy took a joint from her lozenge tin and lit up. Gulls wheeled past, and Vs of geese splashed down.

"Soules will be there," I said. "He knows who I am. When I came down for my morning doughnut, he and Fern were talking about the trial."

"We could go to my friend's, the one I told you about, who's got the place. She won't be there."

"Does she work this early? It's daylight."

"She's got this new gig doing in-calls in the afternoon. The money's more regular and nobody sees her standing on the street."

"It's the same shit." Joy's hooker friend made me angry today. Before, I'd felt curious.

"At least she's doing something. That's more than I can say." Joy squashed down, her knees on the glove box.

"You're going to school, that's something."

"If I make it."

"It's better than what she's doing."

"I don't care. It's a job."

"Sex?"

"It's no different than what you said you did with Ramona and James."

I leaned back, eyes closed, and considered. Joy sounded as ticked off as I was feeling. I wanted to cry. If my dad and I had stayed in Haliburton and Malcolm had been my boyfriend, I'd have the same feelings about sex everybody else did. "They didn't pay me," I said.

"They should've. But it was only sex. It didn't hurt you."

"Yes it did." It still did.

"How?"

"It changed how I felt about Ramona. It tainted it."

"Why?"

"Because of James. She'd never have done those things without James there and she'd never have had him there if she didn't have to keep him happy so she could get her stupid wedding." I spat the word *wedding*.

"Maybe, in the beginning. But you said she became the character with you. She didn't with James."

"So she said. But she was doing it for James, as part of their thing. She was using me. And my feelings for her changed. She wasn't my friend anymore. I wanted her even though I didn't want her, if that makes any sense. And there she was doing things to my body with James there taking pictures. How humiliating."

I flipped the roach into the truck bed and slid the window to an open crack. I pulled out my blouse then tucked it in all the way around. My hands looked chapped, but I didn't feel anything, hot or cold.

"She would've done all that and more if you were alone," Joy said. "But the only way she could get you to do it was in a play. Having you and James there made it more exciting to her. Since you both agreed."

"Alone, we wouldn't have done anything."

I locked eyes with Joy as I edged my tights up from the ankles. My voice sounded resentful. Ramona and I had had sex only because of James. It took me a long time and many books to get that we'd even had sex. In the books I'd read since, sex involved much more than having a penis inside you. Alone, Ramona and I would have stuck to the fairy tales or lost interest. Because I would have stopped her. That's what I'd always believed.

"Something could have happened alone between you," Joy said. "She would have."

"Why do you say that?"

"Because she did. She got into it, too. You could tell from the picture, even though it was hard to see. She was smiling. She was natural. Even if you say and she says she was acting, she did get off on the sex with you."

"Isn't acting part of your job? There was that man you said brought Mary Janes and ruffle panties and you lisped and sucked lollipops and spoke in baby-girl whispers. That had to be an act."

"An act I get paid for. The johns don't take much convincing, and anyway, who did Ramona need to fool?"

"James. Me."

I wouldn't tell Joy, but I hadn't cared whether Ramona got off or not, only that she love me back, as part of the sex, despite it.

"They should have paid you," Joy said.

"Or paid some street girl to do it."

Joy flinched and I met her eye. "Sorry," I said, and she said, "No, it's not that." We sat for a moment and she continued, "Ramona found it more exciting with you."

In Montreal we'd watched the hookers from the window as if they were pretty fish. One time we shared the elevator with a washed-out man and a spotty girl in a mesh halter, her hips bony above tight, low jeans and pumps. I couldn't lock on anything solid in the man, but the girl had the hollow glow of illness. I stared at Jenna, who smiled wide and said "Hello" as if we were at the supermarket. On St. Catherine when a man whispered "How much?" in her ear, I had to pull Jenna away. Sex work tempted us, its improbable taste and its meanness. When Jenna told me one of the hookers took art classes, a wave of cold passed from my breasts to pool in my thighs. I sat in the washroom and cried. Aligning ourselves against the joke of it, the soiled, slutty clothes, the men's dumb-grunt urges, was one thing. I didn't know it then, but what I'd done was too close to what they were doing. I wanted to watch it but I didn't want to make it real.

My legs felt chilly now. I hadn't responded to Jenna's letters since before Christmas. Like Joy she could take in a person whole, and without question. The trial had unsealed the pain and I could write her now, and tell her, too. I started the truck, adjusted the heat, and said, "I've never had sex for money, but I have had sex to get what I wanted. Same thing, I guess. Of course I never did."

"Did what?"

"Get what I wanted."

"Didn't you ever think about being alone with Ramona like that?"

I had, all the time then, but that Ramona acted nothing like Ramona in the basement that February Saturday. She pushed her knuckles into me for James. The fantasy Ramona never did that. In my mind, kissing her was chaste, bodiless.

"Never like that. What I want is never the same as what I get."

Joy turned up her jacket collar and zipped her vest. She tapped her nail against the seat belt buckle.

"What do you want now?"

"That's the problem. I never know what I want until it's too late."

It occurred to me then that I wanted freedom. Myself, without a need for Ramona or Alex. For anyone, woman or man.

With no boats, the lake blended iron into the sky. "There is more," I said now, my nerve rolling into a ball. "You were right."

"Did it happen here? Is that why we came?"

I unclipped my barrette and shook my hair. "Not here," I said. "Not to me."

"Was it with Alex? Ramona and James?"

I sat back and looked over my shoulder toward the bubble-covered tennis court. A minivan coasted down to the Canoe Club gate.

"I don't know as much about murder as you do," Joy continued, "but I think something happened here a few years back. That's not connected, is it?"

"Why don't we go for a walk?"

I put my Docs and work socks on over my tights and

grabbed my notebook. Joy was wading through the long grass. I followed her.

"Am I going the right way?"

I hurdled over the guardrail. My left boot skidded in mud but I caught myself.

"Head toward the boats."

"You never answered my question. Is it James or Alex? Or Ramona?"

I blew air out of my nose. Joy never quit.

She ducked under a sumac then halted at the top of a short bank. Below us the lake curled into a small, pebbly beach. Concrete slabs with twizzlers of rebar crookedly braced the earth. A red metal ladder led down to the water. Pop cans and cigarette packs dotted the mud near a charred log.

"In the summer, there are sailboats," I said. "It's early, but I thought we might see something, a kayak or a canoe, even."

I seized the top of the ladder and lowered myself step by step until I could jump off. The water lapped my Docs. The bouncy soles claimed to be waterproof. I knew from experience that the rest of the boot wasn't.

I sat on the block. Cold concrete nubs dug into me. Joy climbed down then picked up a stick and poked at the water.

"A girl disappeared that same summer," I said, "after what happened with me and Ramona and James. Her name was Agatha Wilson. A man tricked her by saying he would take her picture with members of her canoe club. This canoe club. She lived in Brampton, not that far from Cloud Lake, and she took the bus downtown to meet this man without telling her parents. The bus doesn't come this far, so she met him at the Exhibition Grounds. They found her body in the lake. Not here, further down. But it could have been here. A spot like this would be perfect as long as nobody was around."

"I do remember Agatha Wilson. I was about the same age as her then. That's why it was so scary. My mom wouldn't let me do anything for a while."

"Well, I was eighteen and my dad had no idea what I did."

"They figured out who did it but he killed himself before they could arrest him. Did you know her?" Joy lifted a wet plastic bag with her stick and flung it against a tree.

"No. It's not like that."

I found it easier to talk about Agatha Wilson than myself, despite what I'd spilled on the stand. I held out my notebook. "Read the last part. I wrote it while you were getting the gum."

She took the yellow legal pad and sat beside me, scanning the page.

"Read it. That's all," I said, but she didn't respond. She didn't need to.

While Joy read, I collected garbage bits with her stick and made a heap of pop cans, coffee cups, chip bags, newspaper, candy wrappers, spent firecrackers, condoms, and cigarette packs in the hole of an orange life preserver at the bottom of the ladder. Down here, the cars from Lakeshore made a low machine hum. Pairs of ducks and geese glided along the shoreline.

Then Joy's mouth was on mine, drawing me open, in. Palms pressed my shoulders. Hair threads twined along my eyelashes and cheeks. Tickly, like that night in the box. Like Ramona, but without that pain. More like Alex, if anything. I'd been away one night, but the words *I left him* wouldn't jell. Any kiss with Joy was both an unfinished kiss with Alex and what I should have had with Ramona.

I didn't need to say it, but I did. "You can't tell anybody that part. Not even Aimee."

"Why would I?" Her face fanned open in a smile. "A kiss is a private matter."

"Not that. What you read. I guess because Aimee's your friend. We tell friends things."

"And lovers."

Ropes of hair swished against Joy's down vest. I envied her

waves and wanted my hand in there. My own hair couldn't hold a curl. Wisps skimmed my lips in the breeze. She passed me my notebook.

"Aimee's her street name, remember? She's really Lucy. I bet she'd like to know."

"Lucy?" Joy hadn't said a word about my writing and now she wanted to tell this Lucy person, someone I'd never even met. Why kiss me then — so I'd agree? Anger ballooned in me, glutted my throat.

"Her name's Lucy Rose. She's testifying next week. Do you know who I mean?"

I remembered cigarette smoke and Wayne Stanton sucking on his cheek.

"The star witness?"

"She's the reason I convinced FreeTeach to let me come to the trial. John Soules rents her his basement apartment to give her something more stable. She's been trying to get off the street since James Hawkes got killed."

"She's not the one they're calling 'Jane Doe,' the one who accused them of rape. Officially."

"No, not her. Lucy was working Jarvis last fall, and this couple cruised up and offered her $300 for the night. She did them both in one of those Lakeshore motels, but James came back the next night alone. He met her night after night. He kept paying her but said he was in love with her. Yeah, right. Dumb thing is, she loved him back. She started giving it to him free. He was going to leave his wife for her, she told me."

"Did you believe her?"

"I did when James Hawkes got murdered."

"You should be testifying."

"No way," Joy said, too quickly. I coughed a couple of times but my throat stayed dry. I could have avoided the trial if I'd never identified my photograph. In trying to keep the cops from seeing me as the object of Ramona's jealousy, I'd given up my story. I must have wanted the spotlight. I sagged.

"So Ramona did it — because of Lucy?" *Not me?* My mind

buzzed around this seventeen-year-old Lucy, what Ramona and James had paid her to do. Her choice to run away, live on the street. Sell her body. What if I had run away? I couldn't say my life would have been better — I had gone to university and had a house and husband. But I felt jealous. I'd wanted the memory of me to so enflame Ramona that it drove her to kill her husband. That love, that passion — I had wanted to matter, to be her core thing. To get a response. And I hadn't. Someone else had. Or maybe, as Dr. Highman had suggested, she'd had enough and Lucy offered her a handy excuse.

"I think so."

"Did they act anything out with Lucy? Murders, rapes — anything?" Self-pitying, I sought the slightest edge.

"I wish she'd stayed out of it. They were bad news. Anyone could see it. Sorry. But that's the worst that can happen, to fall in love. Sex is sex. She should have understood that. Ramona Hawkes does."

I agreed, even though Joy hadn't answered my question. The problem, though, as I saw it was that sometimes sex wasn't sex.

Sometimes sex was love.

A thin, mesh light spread over the lake. Slices of red sun rippled between the buildings along the highway.

I sat on the open tailgate while Joy climbed up the ladder from the cove. Her hair swung in the rosy golden light. The shredded cords covered her shoes.

When she got near the truck, Joy said, "Was that Alex? Earlier, by the fence?"

"It was. He came down. I didn't think he would, but he did. We met up afterward. My father came, too. I saw him but he left."

"They both left."

"They both left, true, but Alex waited for me."

"Were you on your way home? Did I delay you? I wanted you to hang out with me so I didn't say anything. You guys looked like you were arguing anyway."

"I guess we were," I mumbled, though our words had felt more like cries of alarm, for a solace neither could find a way to give.

"Are you breaking up with him? You don't seem to be getting along."

I scowled and let myself get defensive to hide my helplessness. "It's more complicated." Asking her what she thought of my story would sound stupid now.

"That's what you said about Ramona. But is it?"

"After five years, you don't walk out."

"People do."

"Not me. You don't know, Joy. And I won't tell you, not about him."

Joy sat and the truck sank. She moved to pull me onto my back but I held fast. Joy had gone to hard, casual places, but for all her gritty views, she saw the blunt sides, not the impossible fluid centre. Her curiosity, her sympathy, and her femaleness made her attractive, but I wasn't done facing myself. I had to say no sometime.

"It was one kiss — a good one; I liked it — but I'm not breaking up with Alex. I'm going home. I never told Alex any of this, do you see that?"

"Fuck him." Joy sprang up and walked off.

"Joy."

"What?"

"Is this why you're here? Did you want this all along?"

Joy came back and said, "I hung around because you feel familiar. You're a writer and you tell the truth. What's not to like? I thought we could have what you thought you had with Ramona. I hoped, anyway."

"It didn't have anything to do with Lucy? Scoping out my story to help her out?"

She squinted. "You don't get it. It's because of Lucy that I get you, but I'm no spy. Not that you could help her anyway. She has to get through this trial."

"She will," I said. Then I blurted, "So you liked what I wrote?"

"I liked what you wrote *about*. We could have fun."

I wanted her to call me a good person and she wanted me to stage a Ramona-game for her. "Leaving takes longer than you think," I said, unsure if I meant Alex or Ramona. Maybe both. My blood pulsed and I stood.

"That's a line. You don't want anyone to get close to you, Pauline."

"It's got nothing to do with want. Maybe I can't."

"Another line. It's what you're afraid of, what you've always been. Alex is safe so you're staying there. Fine. So go."

"I will go, Joy. But Joy —"

A lazy wave eased over the breakwater. Meeting her eyes square on, I took her shoulders in hand, kissed each cheek, and caught her in a close, sinuous hug, the unruly hair finer than imaginable, a texture I'd return to again and again.

chapter 10

When we were nineteen on the East Coast, we'd told ourselves we had a creative bond. Alex was the artist. He'd done a semester in Paris during high school and apprenticed under a local water-colourist who'd said he had talent. I had an urge to draw, and maybe a way of seeing, and the models I'd made for Ramona, so I put away my murder stories and tried to be an artist too.

On Prince Edward Island, we'd parked at the dead end of a wharf road and painted what was in front of us. I watched him mix daubs of burnt umber with titanium white and marvelled at how a line from him could suggest soil against water against sky. My own painting was sloppy and dripping, the bluff dominating the foreground, green stripes angled back to capture early shoots of potato. I loved doing it but soon fell into his dismissal, his experience and strict eye so evident in his own work. Instead I tried my hand at a novel about a sculptor and ended up making the box, art once removed. Alex turned to medicine and, like a car over a hill, his lines vanished, too.

He sat on a stool in my office, a beer in one hand, the other relaxed and open on his lap. I brought in a tray with Earl Grey and shortbread, and lit tea lights. I sat in front of the box.

"You were right," he said.

"I know. About what?"

"That night, two nights ago. It was weird." He told me that when he'd flicked the knife that night, something tucked up inside him. He said he couldn't dislodge the feeling, and when he got to the hospital, the disinfectant smell with its note of blood worked on him until sick flooded his mouth. Then his head tipped, and he couldn't feel why he was there at all.

"The crowd outside the courthouse made me think of you," he said, "so I chanced the speed traps and raced home."

"But I was gone. You knew I went to the trial."

"I figured you wouldn't skip it. I wanted to be waiting for you when you got home. I stayed in. I've never done that here, alone. I spiffed up the house and made a dinner. I thought you'd come home after your little testimony, and we could make it up. Reset and go back to before."

"Before what?"

"Before this Ramona person."

"She got here ahead of you," I said. "That's the thing. And my testimony was hardly little."

"I know that now. I thought you'd be giving some times and locations. Where you were the night of. Quick and incriminating. Now I see we haven't had any life without Ramona under the surface."

He said he'd woken up fascinated with me, so he put on my University of Guelph sweatshirt and went to the post office and bought the paper at the Lucky Dollar the way I did, only my story was front page. When he read it, what was inside him tucked up even further, so he tried to picture me in a teenage friendship with the woman on trial for murdering her husband, and he could do it and make some sense of it. He said when he went into my office, he saw the black cone like a lopsided space shuttle and found it "unimpressive," not beautiful or contrived in any meaningful way, and he felt the same blunt frustration that my murder stories gave him. He said he hated that I'd made the sculpture of a character from my novel, that my writing was "interactive" and "experiential," that I didn't tell a story in the distilled way he believed I should but put in the whole of me, that I brought the inside out while he craved design.

As he spoke, I kept my back to the door. A peace settled on us.

"Is it the box you hate or the fact that I built it?"

"Both. And why you built it. You're a writer." He coloured. I took his hand.

"You've never said that before." I felt tender toward him now, and bitter. Warmth crept up my legs.

"You're good. I don't tell you because you already know."

"That's a shitty reason. Also, how do you know I know? We've never talked about it."

"You're confident in it. You're doing it. If you thought — or even suspected — you weren't good, why would you do it?"

"Maybe because I hope I'm good but I won't know until I've done it or until someone tells me."

"Too complex," he said. "You're good, now you know."

"By the way," I said, "I scrapped that novel a while ago. All that's left is the box. I'm writing this new story. I might even be done."

"Can I see it?"

"It's not your kind of thing. That's what you said before."

"It is if you wrote it." Shy, I moved next to him and let him sling his arm over my shoulder.

"Later then. Maybe I'll read it to you and you can cover your ears during the scary parts. Are you going back?"

"To the hospital? I could. Dr. Augustin left a message. He wants to meet me tomorrow. I could duck over there before you start the cross, explain about your trial and ask for a leave because of extreme stress. What more can I do? I should have talked to him before."

"That's nice," I said, shaky at his generous heart, overwhelmed. Best to change the subject. "Do you think you'll paint again? You've never said."

"Maybe I will," Alex said. "Don't pay me too much mind, though. That's part of the problem. Being called artist and good makes it hard to be or do anything but what people responded to in the first place. There was no life there for me and in medicine there is. And even though I don't like it, and I don't like having to have it explained to me, there is life in this thing you've built — and in the stories you write."

"Even though they're about murder?'

He laughed. "I guess I want that life for myself."

"You have it," I said. "We do. That's what that night was all about."

"Which?"

"That night we played surgery."

"That's your problem right there."

"What?"

"Play. You call it play."

"What would you call it?"

"Real." He held his hand over my mouth before I could interrupt. "Yes, we were playing a game. But you pushed it farther than I wanted. That's what Ramona and James did with you. Only then, you were playing a game and they broke the rules and made it real."

"But you liked it when I pushed you."

"I liked cutting you? No, I didn't, even if it looked that way. The next morning, when you got up, I pretended to sleep. I couldn't face you. You didn't like it when Ramona pushed you too far either."

"It was the camera I didn't like. Having the camera there made it real. The story's out there now, I can't escape it. James, Ramona, they could always look at the pictures and get turned on. It wasn't fair. It was as if they owned part of me after I was gone and they could use it — me — whenever they wanted. I had no say. Now I've seen the photo, too. God. The thought of them looking at it, for sex, repulses me. I shouldn't say it but I'm glad he's dead. I'm glad she killed him."

"She can't look either. The cops have them now."

"Yes, but *they* can see. Everyone at the goddamn trial saw. How do I know Stanton didn't make a copy for his own collection?"

"Not everyone's like that. He's a good man. You said that before."

"Yes, but what do I know? Look at the friends I chose."

"Look at the man you chose." His face tilted, half shadowed against yellow light, he watched me, afraid, maybe, that I'd take it the wrong way. I'd always thought he'd chosen me. I wondered if he knew. My rage settled.

Safe, he cupped my knees. "And who do you love?"

"You know."

"Yes."

We set our hands together. His thumb rubbed my wrist. Then I looped my arms around his shoulders and slid up. He rocked back with me in the wavering light, my cheek in the dip where his chest drummed, and we rested.

In bed, we spooned and I said, "A camera would change what we did, too."

"How?"

"It makes us aware of what we make together, moment to moment. It's life, like you said. That's why you're right, it's not a game. I can show you."

"Whatever it takes," Alex said. "You know that."

I pulled up, ready to jump out of bed. I didn't want to sleep. He got his arm around my shoulder and held me close.

"We will," he said. "When it's normal again."

"It's normal now. It's good."

"Yes, it is. But that's now. Let's keep it this way, let it last awhile."

"After the trial, right? After I'm done. "

"Yes. And then some."

In my dream that night I sat writing at a desk in a prison. I don't know what put me there, but the desk and my writing at it were part of the punishment. My guard was Joy, only she didn't look like herself, and her name was J. The prison looked like a bare, white apartment. My desk had a window behind it. J had fallen in love with a murderer. I could see that he was a murderer, but J didn't know and didn't believe me when I told her. Maybe I was wrong. Her lover visited her and she forgot about me. He had no hair and rubbery red neck wrinkles. He darted around the room, dashed at me like a dog. I slipped free as best I could, stuck as I was at the desk. He glanced at the window. He would come back and enter there. He would get me. In time.

I woke up cold, arms over my head, and scared. The window was open, the curtains parted. Leaves swished and sighed. A wind chime tinkled. Sparrows prattled. The dream had held a message about my writing, but not a good message. What had put me in prison? The story. I'd loved writing it. It made no sense to punish me with writing. How do you punish a person by giving her what she wants? Love had sideswiped the guard. She couldn't protect me. I'd have to leave my story and jump. Or fight. I didn't know if I could. I shut the window and drew the curtains.

"Morning," Alex said from his dark side of the bed.

"You up?"

"I am. Bad dream?"

"Yeah."

"Tell me."

I lay on my back. "It's a long one. Why don't I read to you instead? My notes are over there."

He shifted onto his side. "I'm ready."

"It's about Mona."

"Mona?"

"Ramona."

Only yesterday, I'd shown these same words to Joy. As I read, the experience floated out of me like smoke. Happy, I let it go.

I remember it was February, the second Saturday. I remember that because it was close to Valentine's Day. I didn't have a boyfriend but I didn't care. I was too old for the soppy stuff. I was eighteen. I had Ramona.

chapter 15

I opened my eyes. I was lying in the basement workroom at 17 Covered Wagon Trail. Handcuffs looped my wrists through a ring bolted to the wall. Pain drilled my armpits. My stomach groaned. My eyes watered. The wine was wearing off. I stretched a leg. It dragged, the movement sloppy.

"Let me," James said.

"No," Ramona said. "We agreed." She knotted the belt on her kimono. Without makeup her skin looked like freckled rubber.

"I know," James said. "But look at her. You can go upstairs or stay. I don't give a fuck."

"No way. We made a deal."

"Tough shit. It's for here. It doesn't mean anything."

"Don't be so sure."

Ramona meandered upstairs. I watched her with an awful mix of longing and chary relief. I wanted her, but maybe James alone was the lesser evil. He came over and snuck his arm around my waist. His shirt had a horsy warmth and smelled like soap. I shifted. The pain backed off then surged, keener now. He eased the tape off my mouth. It made a snap like paper ripping.

"It's all right. She's gone."

· I swallowed. My cheeks felt gummy, scoured. I opened my mouth, but I had nothing to say. I hitched myself closer to the wall.

"I'm not going to hurt you. Neither is she. We wanted those photos because that's our guy's pathology. He likes dirty photos of his wife fondling their kidnap victims. Actually, there's a lot more he'd like, but of course we wouldn't do anything against your will. You can understand why we couldn't tell you all the details before. As I said, I'm not into violence, but we did have to play it up to get as close as we could to the real thing. We did a good job, don't you think?"

He stroked my face with a hairy knuckle and whispered, "Little girl."

A bubble rolled in my throat. My chest burned. I wished I could throw up on him.

"If she hurt you, she didn't mean it. She wants to please me. Like you."

James had let what he wanted fool him, as I had. I stayed with the surprise of it, the disgust.

"But what she said —" I hated that I sounded like I cared. I hated that I did, but there it was. If I could get into my clothes, if we could move forward into the day, I could get Ramona back to before.

"That's talk. She cares about you. I do too, but not like her. She wouldn't have included you in this if she didn't. You are glad we did include you, aren't you? We didn't go too far? You could have stopped us any time."

After a moment I shook my head. I hadn't thought to stop them. Stupid. I hadn't thought I could. Was this what he meant about not going against my will? It wasn't right.

"I won't hurt you or do anything to you that you don't want. If what we did today was too much, we won't do it again. We'll keep it between us."

"I don't know what you mean."

"Let's say there was some truth behind what Ramona said. Maybe you do want me a little. Maybe she is mad at you. That's okay. Feelings are okay. But we shouldn't rub her face in it. She'll do anything for me, but she gets what she wants. If she finds out about this going any further between you and me, she will make sure you are hurt. She doesn't mean to, but if you look at what happened today, you can see she can't help herself. That's how she is."

James had seized on the parts of my act that said I wanted him. I asked again what he meant.

He stepped back and traced my eyebrow. His eyes never left mine, despite my exposed body. He said, "There is something between us. I doubt there is something between you and Ramona. She acted the way she did to please me and hurt you because she senses what you and I have. I'm saying maybe we should do something about this connection ourselves. But keep her out of it. To be fair to her."

"That doesn't sound fair," I said, cheered that he hadn't noticed what Ramona and I had.

"If she doesn't know about it," James said, "it won't hurt her. She wants all those things she said earlier, she wants me to go all the way and do things to you against your will. Which I could. There's a point I can go to, which is pretty far, and stop myself when it's time. You have that point, too. But why don't we try it on our own."

"Because you'd rather be with me?"

"Because Ramona doesn't want me to be with you unless I force you, and I'd rather you agree. I don't think this worked for you. Let's find something that does. Do you want to try?"

He whisked my hair off my face. My joints ached. I kept my thighs crossed. My face dry, gluey — had I cried? At first I didn't care about my body, but then I did, so I asked him to cover me and he took his top shirt off and wrapped me. He didn't undo the cuffs, though, but I didn't ask. Dizziness heaved, and I had to squint to see his face with the light behind him.

With James there, Ramona had turned nasty. She'd called me names and mangled my skin and probably covered me with scratches and bruises. I'd submitted to the game and now she had left me naked and chained for James because she catered to his wants. I had a hard time believing she was acting. She wasn't.

My body had sold me out. I *had* wanted Ramona, but not here, not like this. I loathed her. I loathed myself. Sore, I craved her bullying hands, but alone, maybe on the waterbed, not here on the hard-cornered workshop bench with James's Polaroid eye sliding over me. My body didn't know what it wanted. Time to stop listening to it. Ramona had deserted me here. I would desert her right back. If I could break her and James up in the process, all the better.

I released a long sigh. An ending where the kidnapped victim stole the kidnapper from his wife had never struck me as possible — or desirable.

It didn't matter what I had with James. Ramona had set us up. Now, when James kissed me again, I made myself limp. This kiss should not be happening, particularly after this afternoon, this day, however long they had kept me in their basement workshop. This kiss did not belong to me. I should not allow it. But how could I not? I had nowhere to go.

James clenched his jaw and led with teeth and firm tongue. My throat closed at his fecal coffee and bleach taste. Whereas Ramona's mouth and insistent hands had coaxed a dormant current free, James's mouth left me clotted and thick as if stuffed with mushy paper. At the prospect of Ramona coming down and catching me, I gnawed my cheeks. Her wanting James and me to do this — or worse, not caring what we did — didn't occur to me. This was not about symmetry, nor soulmates, nor karmic destiny, nor any of Ramona's versions of an ideal couple. It was about a hole in the middle of me that started when I was born and grew until my mother left and the edges turned necrotic.

I'd read true crime after true crime in pursuit of the potent moment between murderer and victim before life ended. In James's kisses, I hit the familiar cord that tied off love. My body urged me into pain, incited me against Ramona, beyond her. I met his mouth with a suckling fury. *Fuck her if she comes down.* I hoped she would. He didn't touch me. Even shackled and nude on the wood table, I could believe I was part of it, that sex wasn't all of it. In that torpid tonguescrew, the moment counted most.

We kissed for less than a minute. James unlocked the handcuffs and massaged my wrists. "The outfit is there on the floor," he said. "Wait, and I'll get your regular clothes." He left.

I swung my legs over the table's edge. My feet dangled in the distance, like somebody else's. My fingers moved but slowly, as if swollen. My arms felt wrung out. I slid the panties up high so the gusset met my vulva then swiped the fabric with my thumb. No blood. They hadn't cleaned me. The earlier wetness must have been urine.

I detested clinical terms like urine, vulva, gusset — but they kept repeating in my mind, mocking and protecting me. I hooked the brassiere, waited, then put on the ensemble. I had no reason not to go up, but enough fear lingered to root me.

Ramona came down, not James, and without my clothes.

She waved at me to follow, as if we'd performed a play like *Rapunzel* or *Hall of Mirrors*. I went with her to her bedroom. My clothes lay on the bed.

"Do you mind if I stay while you change? Or do you want some privacy?" She was using her office voice.

"No, it's okay." I stood in the doorway.

Grey light outlined the drawn curtains. The clock radio said 6:13. We'd started at 9:00 Saturday morning, half an hour after my dad had left for Haliburton. I could have stayed in the basement overnight. The wine — drugs? — had wiped my sense of time. If it was Sunday I had to hurry. Dad was coming home for dinner.

As if on cue, Ramona said, "Hank — your dad — called."

"What for?"

"To check on you. He loves you. Maybe he missed you."

"Me?"

"It happens. Some parents like their children. I told him you just left."

"Is he coming home?"

"Not until tomorrow."

Saturday. Events that had seemed to take days had lasted only hours. Pain crackled my head. I turned away to change bras then pulled my panties and jeans up before taking off the skirt. I sat beside her, clothed but barefoot. The waterbed rolled with me. I suppressed a dry heave. She didn't talk. Neither did I.

In the mirror, next to Ramona, I slouched, square and plaid, my eyes, with the lamp behind, purpled into a hollowed-out bandit mask. Everything about me plain, even my hair, which, though she had once said it held a "mahogany shine," was mouse-turd brown. Beside me, Ramona's changeling, not-beautiful face, compelling and radiant, shifted in shadow. An elemental shrewdness seized her features for one ravenous moment. Then she stood. The waterbed rippled. It was over.

I didn't see James. Our goodbye was swift and devoid of promises. Then I was plodding through curdling slush toward Hartley Horse. Nothing could touch me. With each step, the seams of my jeans chafed my skin. I dipped my mitten in a puddle and brought it to my face with a firm squeeze. I wouldn't miss her. I wouldn't feel guilt. I would think of him. She didn't want me anyway. If she found out James wanted to create murder/victim scenarios alone with me, she might call off the wedding. It didn't matter whether she hated me. I didn't care if I ever saw her again. She should pay for hurting me. She'd denied what was real between us. Now, I had to wait to hear from James.

I wished I had Burt with me. Dad had taken him north. I turned and headed out to Kennedy Road. My face dripped, my cheeks hot in the wake of the tape's scratchy residue. I wanted to walk and never stop. My bootslaps reassured me. The streetlights shone. Cars rushed past. Nobody else was walking. Nobody here walked.

Angry, I felt brave. Honoured, too, and different — from Ramona and from anything my mother could have imagined for me. Fierce and vindicated, I would say to her, "See. This is what happens to girls whose mothers leave. I didn't choose this. You did. You made me bad."

My walk got cocky. Then I drooped. That wasn't it. I'd thought I had a friend, more, and I didn't. I turned around and went home and lay in a hot bath, hands prayerful between my thighs. I made myself think of James and all the things that spun inside me now, things that would build me, my own things that nobody else ever got to know.

My tailbone throbbed. I checked myself all over, but Ramona's pinches and digs had left no marks. I went to bed early and woke up and missed Burt. I watched *Davey and Goliath* and *Wild Kingdom* and did Chemistry homework and made a mushroom soup casserole. Dad ate more than half even though he'd had a burger on the way home.

He asked why I winced when I got up from the couch and believed me when I said I'd fallen getting off the bus. I left the room and ran a bath, my fifth since I got back from Ramona's. He didn't ask about that. His kind of love believed what it was shown. My tailbone throbbed and would for months to come. He mentioned it once more, to say, "Tailbones take a long time to heal," and I saw him then as a man who could hurt a woman with harsh desire. I didn't like looking at his hands after that.

I stopped going to Venus Video. The owner never called. Dad praised me for acting like a real teenager. I spent most of my time at the library.

I reread every true crime I could find and felt superior to the victims who couldn't outsmart their captors, outmanoeuvre the pain and stay alive. I had survived.

Sometimes Ramona's taste coated my mouth. Sometimes my thighs clenched against her raw push. I made myself re-place Ramona with an image of Malcolm holding me on the trailer bunk and that comfort. *Strawberry Peck Forever.* His name for me. I busied myself with homework. I took down my Beatles poster and Lennon banner and painted my walls black. My dad never came home right after work. Burt and I often had the place to ourselves. Burt took to sleeping with one possessive leg flopped across my foot.

I graduated from Western Secondary without having made a single friend there. I had high grades from the studying I'd done since Valentine's. Impressed, my dad agreed to help with university as long as I worked. I got accepted by all three of my choices. I picked Guelph and registered for the fall. I got my old job back at Venus Video.

Ramona never came into the store and I could believe nothing had happened, except it had. There were three of us there. James had taken photos. What had happened had happened to me. It wasn't a crime, at least it didn't feel that way, and I didn't see it that way, though any sensible person would advise me to tell my dad, maybe the police.

Most wouldn't understand my need to see James again. But I would see him, though I didn't know when or how.

Our game hadn't ended.

Only, without Ramona, it became a twosome once more.

On August 1, there was a manila envelope in the mailbox with my name on it, no address. The handwriting had a spidery slant I couldn't place.

Inside I found a typed letter and a newspaper clipping. I read the letter first.

> *Dear Pauline:*
> *My feelings haven't changed. I wanted to see you one last time before the wedding, but it had to be right. I didn't want to make a mistake. But now I've had an idea. Read the article, and if you're willing, we can meet on Wednesday by the Dufferin Gate so*

I can take your picture by the lake.
We can go from there if you like.

There was no signature, but I didn't need one. On the back, a postscript asked me to write yes or no at the bottom and put the envelope back in my mailbox before I went to bed.

The article was about Agatha Wilson, the missing girl. Agatha was younger than me, not even in high school, blonde and dark-eyed like Ramona. She wore a ponytail and a life jacket and held a paddle in both hands. She'd disappeared a couple of days earlier. Nobody knew what happened. James would have to invent what he wanted to do here. We would create it together.

I wrote *yes* and left the envelope in the mailbox. I forgot about it for the rest of the night and worked on a jigsaw puzzle of the Grand Canyon. I'd lost my urge to write plays and make models. It surprised me to find the envelope there in the morning and again when I got home from work. Then I caught on that James might use the same envelope for his next letter.

This time there was only one sheet. The typed instructions were direct and clear.

On Wednesday, my day off, I rode the same buses downtown that Ramona and I had taken the summer before. I even bought a sugar-coated doughnut at Kirby's. I carried the folded instructions inside my purse. James and Ramona's wedding was in ten days. No invitation had come to our house. James was taking a bar admissions course at Osgoode Hall on Queen Street. His class ended at 12:30. He planned to come out the double doors at 12:35. I should watch for him from Nathan Phillips Square then take the Queen streetcar and the Dufferin bus to the Dufferin Gate bridge by the Exhibition Grounds where he would drive by in his maroon Escort and pick me up. I should not let him see me at Osgoode. If he didn't come out by 12:40, I should go home and we'd meet another time, if at all. I wore no costume, only jeans with a sleeveless denim blouse and runners. My shoulder-length hair swung in a ponytail double-wrapped with a neon pink scrunchy. I could be any girl, anyone at all, in the streams of people strolling across Nathan Phillips Square. I read the writing on each side of the Winston Churchill statue and walked the perimeter of the fountain pool under the arches. The sun hit my face as I stared up at the elliptical City Hall buildings. Gull shrieks dopplered around me. A wire loop on a flag rattled against the pole. I sat on a bench heaped underneath with copper beer cans and oily napkins. The wood seared my thighs. I positioned myself behind a planter of small maples, browned roses, and drooping purple coneflowers where I could see Osgoode's side door across the lawn, and I waited for him. He knew I was there. He was coming to find me. I had some idea, but didn't know in the end who he'd be, what he'd do, how far he'd go. I did know I would go as far.

"What do I do now?" I asked. I crouched on the hot car floor. My sunglasses had fallen off.

He didn't answer. Sunlight blades sliced the wide bench seat.

I crawled up.

His hand shot out and knocked my head against the glove compartment. My jeans gouged my crotch, the backs of my knees. One foot bent backward. The car smelled of melting plastic.

I waited. Surely a kidnapper didn't sit and watch the sky through the tinted stripe on his window while his victim huddled under the dash. His big khaki knee filled my vision. He wore a cream shirt and a braided leather belt. Green aviator sunglasses. A dusting of chinstubble.

He'd turned the engine off when we arrived and rolled up his window. Earlier my sneakers had squeaked against the rubber floor mat and he'd directed me to take them off. I'd taken off my sockettes, too, and placed them inside my shoes, which he lifted with two fingers and dropped in the back seat.

There should be music. How would a scared girl with a real kidnapper act? Some would try to escape. Some would do what the kidnapper asked so they could get away. This kidnapper hadn't asked anything, though.

I moved up again and caught his hand on my face. His palm stuck to my lips and pinched one nostril shut. The other nostril wheezed against his flesh with its pencil and orange peel smell. When he shoved, my spine bumped the dash, but I was wedged too firmly to move. I braced my arms and got first one leg then the other up until my shoulders propped the windshield.

"Get the hell down," he said. Silver and a red wedge flashed.

He snatched my waistband and turned me onto my back in a clatter of keys and legs. His hands circled my throat and contracted, the Swiss Army knife a cool lump behind my ear. His tanned lips made an even line. My left arm twisted under, right hand catching his shirt sleeve. My throat bruise-dry, mouth-breaths like chair legs scraping brick as I tried to back up to the door, but he plunged and kneed my legs open. I turned, thigh-cramped, but his weight checked me. When I reached for his belt, he swatted my hand away and flung the sunglasses swinging from one ear into the back. Crescent eyes carved his sweatface.

He bunched up my shirt and pulled my bra to the sides. He knuckle-tweaked my nipples and it hurt, but my bent neck against the door hurt more. He undid my jeans and I thrashed my arm free. He touched himself and growled. With his other hand he got my jeans and panties to my knees. One palm landed on my neck again while the other hand moved up and down inside his pants. He said, "Fuck," and growled. He dropped his pants and boxers halfway like mine and levered my knees up using the crotch of my jeans. My back arched over the armrest; the seat belt buckle poked my bare tailbone and that pain, old now, shot up pure. He parted me with harsh fingers and loomed, his cream shirt buttoned, gelled hair tips bowed against the grey felt ceiling. My body gave up nothing. Without Ramona there, I stayed dry and closed. I had a moment's blush at my wetness coating her hand that cold morning in the basement. Now, in the car, James yanked his penis while his fingers pried me open, but nothing entered. He said, "Fuck" again, then buckled his belt and got out of the car.

I slapped my legs together, hitched up my jeans, and stuffed myself back into my bra. I leaned out the door and retched. My throat burned and spittle slicked my hand.

The car was parked in sedge and switch grass with nearby jack pines and cottonwoods. Sand and the lake's blue weave washed the area from the grass to the white horizon. James caught a branch with his left hand and swung himself over a ridge.

I hurried after him barefoot on the desiccated grass and called his name. Spit clogged my throat. I cleared it and called again. He hadn't given me an alias for the kidnapper, but I wasn't playing anymore. Sticks poked my soles as I broke into a trot. I hopped over the edge, staggered briefly in the gravelly sand, then ran full out, dodging logs and weed tufts until I got close enough to slam my fist against his back. I grabbed his damp shirt, half wound my arm up, and hit his muscle again.

He stood idle but didn't turn to face me. He had the peppery smell of fresh sweat.

"Why did you stop?" My voice burbled. "Wasn't I believable?"

He dipped his head. I remembered the sly white strip when I first met him last summer. An even brown coated his neck now.

"Pauline, no. It's not that," he said in his regular voice. He reached back for my arm and loosened my grip. He took both wrists, on his face a heavy questioning. Behind him a dog cantered, head high, teeth chopping a log, toward a man in a fishnet undershirt. The man reached for the log and the dog veered, tucked its head, and charged in a crazed, water-shedding blitz toward the sedge. It skidded, tossed the log, and watched, front legs wishbone-shaped, as the wood dropped on the sand. I hadn't brought Burt to the beach for a long time.

"It's not the same with you," James said. "I can act this kind of thing out with Ramona. I could even do it with you two together. It's not right this time. Maybe it's that we don't know the story. They haven't caught that guy yet. They haven't even found Agatha Wilson's body. So we're out here trying to make up a scenario. Something new has to happen between you and me because we don't know enough about Agatha Wilson to imitate her. I'm not prepared to let something happen here. I made a mistake."

I fumbled at his belt loops with hooked fingers. As he lifted my hands away, I said, "There's other things we can do," though I had no reason. James and Ramona were getting married next weekend, and I hadn't come here to have sex, though I would have. We had come here to play-act murderer and victim. I had liked the struggle but didn't like to feel thwarted. "We could act out another story," I said. "One where we know the ending, like Starkweather or Bundy."

He bounced my wrists lightly and said, "This isn't what I wanted." An edge to his voice.

"What about what I wanted?"

"I can't help you there." He let my hands fall, lifted a foot, and took off his shoe. "I don't know why they're called sandals," he said and poured out a grey stream. "They're shit in the sand." He put the shoe on then did the same with the other.

"What time is your bus ticket?" he asked. "I should get you to the station. Maybe you can catch an earlier one."

I crossed my arms. Even though Jim lived around the corner, I wouldn't ask him for a ride home. I followed him to the car. This time, the sun-fried grass flayed my soles.

chapter 16

"What was she like?"

"Who, Ramona? I told you."

"Your mother."

"That's all you have to say?"

"You never talk about her."

"That's what the stories are for."

"The stories, yes, but I assume your mother wasn't a murderer."

"Why?"

"News like that you'd tell me straight."

"She wasn't. But she left."

"You must miss her."

On my knees, I parted the bedroom curtain. A tender pink splayed across the grey sky. I took a breath and a corrosive burn flared against my ribs. Alex's face humble, drained. A light rose in him, too.

"I can't believe I told you that story and all you can do is ask about my mother."

"You're doing a good thing, Pauline, putting this bloody woman away."

"Funny, it doesn't feel like that's what I'm doing."

"Let me talk. It doesn't matter what happens to her. She doesn't matter. I don't care about her, or her dead, impotent husband. Nobody does. You shouldn't either."

I hadn't seen it before but he was right. Whatever James was doing, he wasn't having sex. Not with me, anyway, and maybe not with Ramona. Maybe in Lucy he'd found someone who made him hard. I didn't feel sorry for him.

"You're right. I'd stop caring if I could."

"You can. You must hate her. You must look at her on the stand and simply hate her."

"Maybe. Mostly I feel nothing. It's me I hate."

"Don't. No."

"Easy enough to say. Whether she goes away or not, no matter what comes out of me on the stand, I've got her poison in me."

"We'll work on that."

"How?"

"I'm a doctor, remember? I'm full of antidotes."

"Nice." I shook myself free of his hands and got up. "Very nice." I acted as if I didn't like his pawing but I did. I liked it very much.

We'd run out of plums so Alex ate a kiwi in the car, brown fuzz and all. Then he held my hand across the emergency brake. Though we'd left early we hit a bottleneck at King Road and idled our way into the city. We didn't talk, and it felt peaceful, a quiet, held-in breath. Alex let go of my hand to shift then picked it up again. At the Bev's Donuts on Black Creek he sent the woman — Kris, he introduced her as; she smiled and said, "You must be Pauline" — back for an extra order of his usual. Coffee speeds up my heart but

I sucked this one right down. He parked under the hospital. He showed me how to get to the street. Then I left him to his meeting with Dr. Augustin and walked over to the courthouse alone.

I scanned the lineup. When I didn't see Joy, I ducked my head and hurried inside. Outside 7-2, I read Cindy Fist's column. It didn't surprise me. My testimony validated what she had suspected all along about Ramona Hawkes. Today, she came out crowing.

It's not consent if they're raping you
By Cynthia Fist
Toronto Telstar

Toronto – There are terms for people like the Hawkeses. An erotophonophiliac gets aroused while attempting to kill someone. A biastophiliac gets aroused by the idea of being raped. We can call Ramona Hawkes a narcissist, an anti-social psychopath, or a murderess, but we can't undo her damage. Her tastes are as vile as her husband's were, yet she's all the more despicable because she's tried to get us to sympathize with her as his victim. Sorry, dear. Not buying it.

At times, Pauline Brown disturbs me more. The person inside is using the body, but she's not at home. She has smooth, practised movements, but almost too much so. A weird combination of a body possessed by a demon and the humanoid robot from *Star Trek: The Next Generation*.

I hope she doesn't think she had a part in what happened. Being drugged and raped, verbally abused and even hit doesn't constitute consensual sex, whether you're a biastophiliac or not, no matter how much you claim you set it up or enjoyed it. Pauline Brown was a teenager. She may have her own issues, but she can't deny what went on in that basement workshop.

What Cindy revealed at the end of the article disturbed me most. The previous day she had gone to St. Mary's Hospital and found that Alexander Hazen Gates Shore hadn't shown up for his internship in the Emergency Room for two days. "St. Mary's," she reported, was "checking into it." Cindy signed off with a plea to Alexander Shore to come forth and tell her his story.

I paced the hall, furious. When the escalator brought Cindy up, alone, I met her at the top. She carried a raincoat and wore a tapestry vest over a shirt with the collar standing up. She held a travel mug.

"I'm ready for that coffee now, Cindy," I said.

Her chin gathered like fabric into a smile. She looked ready for me, wary, too vivid. She glanced around the hallway. A few people sat outside the courtroom door.

"Detective Stanton's not here yet," I said.

"No, I know. Listen," she said, "I just filled my mug but let's go back down and I'll buy you one. You haven't got much time. They'll need you soon."

We were alone in the elevator all the way to ground level.

"I'd rather take you outside," Cindy said. "The cafeteria here serves crayon water, and there're too many ears."

We took a table near the back of a Bev's Donuts with a box of Do'nubbins between us.

"There's not much I can ask you now. I'm not prepared, and you're testifying. I take it you're ready to talk, though? Give me your side, what you can't say on the stand."

The coffee burned my lips. "You don't understand the effect your column has on me."

"Of course I do." Her words raced out of her. "I'm supporting you, like I do all of the victims. Ramona's a monster and you know it. I say what I see and the paper pays me." She wore the look of neutral sympathy I imagined psychiatrists used.

"You weren't far off with that robot comment. That's what I

feel like," I admitted. I reminded myself she'd ticked me off and held up my hand before she could say more supportive things. "But Alex, my husband, he's what I want to talk to you about." Today the word *husband* sounded ruined, stained, inappropriately intimate. Maybe I was done saying it, at least until I had one.

"I don't know anything. That's what I said in my article." Cindy sat back, her face closed.

"But you do. You know he didn't show up for work. Tell me what you did to find him."

"You didn't know he was missing?" Her fingers drummed the table, probably itching for a pen.

"Can you promise not to use what I say? Can we talk off the record? Because I've had enough exposure and this isn't about Ramona, so who cares."

Cindy shrugged off her coat and took the lid off her cup. The ends of her red, oval nails had chipped. She leaned across the table, conspiratorial. "I'll help you with your husband if you'll give me material for my book. Simple as that."

I chewed on a Do'nubbin as I talked. "You've called me some cold names. Why would I do that?"

"Because he's important to you and you can't find him and maybe I can."

"He's not missing. But even if he were, it's not your business." I shut up then. In her article Cindy had questioned the coincidence of my husband walking off the job on the day I testified at a murder trial.

"Hey, I'm a reporter, doing what I do. So he's back now and he's told you what he's told you. Maybe he told you he watched you testify. But let's say he did go missing. How would you have known? You stayed at a hostel overnight. You've been down here, busy with the trial. Are you two having problems?"

She was right. She probably always was. The urge to drag her to the hospital, rub Alex in her face, choked me. Was that what Alex was? Proof to the world that I could hold a man — meet him and love him and keep him close? Maybe. But not anymore. Surely not now.

"Your book will be good," I said to her. "But I won't help you with it." *You'll have to wait for mine if you want the real story.* My shoulders quaked.

"Thank you. I am good at what I do. You should let me help." Cindy held out the box with the last Do'nubbin, a Hawaiian sprinkle, and I took it. We'd popped them like crazy while we talked.

"You're reporting on a trial, not my life. Alex is not part of this."

"He is, because of you."

"Stop it, then. Leave him out of it. And believe what I say on the stand. Your opinions are fire. If you don't watch it, they'll burn up everything that's real."

She sucked in her cheeks and said, "I disagree."

"I know people want you to do what you do. Heck, I wanted you to do it, too — when it wasn't about me. I don't like you using my life to make your living. Nobody would."

"I'll pay you for your story. Maybe you're missing that part of it."

I drained the rest of my coffee and stood to go. "I'm not, and no. My story's worth more than that. What's left of it anyway. Goodbye, Cindy," I said and walked off before she could reply.

On Friday, April 24, 1992, at 10:12 a.m., after Justice Larraby had knocked on his private door to signal his entrance, the registrar had called, "Order in the court, all rise!", and the court had bowed to the judge, I took my place on the witness stand. I didn't look for Joy. Or my dad. Maybe he'd come back? It didn't matter. Even Alex, he'd get here when he could. Buttressed, I stared at Ramona centre stage in her Plexiglas box as I spoke. When Bill Witherson blocked my view, I craned my neck. Ramona leaned with her chin on her right hand, two fingers poised against her cheek. Her tongue rolled like a ball bearing inside her lips. As I drew air down deep, caustic pain slathered my chest. *This is me, mine.* I invited it in, sat in its fire as Ramona blew up bigger and bigger. Her nothingness filled the room, the air that fed my stuck, cankered heart, the big fool thing I was parading for the world. Oh God, my air.

I turned away and let my breath flow true. I never looked at her again.

Bill Witherson's robe rustled as he strode to the lectern with a practised lankiness. His questions came out rapid-fire, his impatience with me clear.

I recoiled. I'd hoped he'd play Mr. Nice Guy the way he had with Lyndsey Franklin, but I was ready for him. I held my own.

Yes, I told him, Ramona and James and I had played a game that Saturday in February on Covered Wagon Trail. I had given Ramona reason to believe I had consented. I had consented. I'd also changed my mind. Ramona and James had bound me and given me enough wine to get me drunk. Drugs had fogged my memory. I hadn't consented to take drugs. There was no way to prove Ramona and James had given me any. I hadn't told my father. I hadn't called the police. I'd never told another soul.

"Do you believe you were raped, Ms. Brown?"

"I didn't say that."

"Do you?"

Justice Larraby leaned over and said, "Answer the question."

"I'm not sure who you're referring to, sir."

"Do you believe you were raped by either Mr. or Mrs. Hawkes or both?"

"I believe I may have been, yes."

"Were you raped? Yes or no."

I caught myself scratching my temple and dropped my hand into my lap. A yes meant, what? That Ramona had assaulted me. That she'd forced me to do things sexually that I hadn't agreed to do. Much was wrong with what had happened, but I couldn't pin the couple with the damning term. Maybe I was feeling real love, finally, or no-love. I wanted Ramona to go away, the trial, too. It had invaded me. I didn't want the responsibility. Let someone else put her away. Let Lucy. I felt weak, strained. I would keep mum about the worst parts with James. Revenge no longer mattered. James was dead. Ron had told me to address my answers to the judge. I met Justice Larraby's aspic gaze as I let go of Ramona's fate.

After I'd first seen Ramona on the cover of the *Toronto Telstar*, I often pictured her in prison. They'd have put her in segregation first. She had a high profile and needed protection. Some of the victims had been young enough to cause a problem. Young enough.

In my picture, she moves her mattress to the floor by the door and stares up. Red streaks flower on the ceiling. Bloodstems. Her scars itch against the green sweats. Her arms goose-pimple in the pink T-shirt. Time to think, surely, the fluorescent light on sixteen hours, and every sound, every footfall, scream, moan, curse, amplifies through the cool slit where the door meets the floor. Three times a day, a guard passes meals and books through a slot. She likes murder mysteries, Agatha Christie, P.D. James. She reads a book a day.

She complies with the showers, lets the two guards in Seg escort her down the short hall. She slips out of the thick cotton underwear and steps into the stall. Her skin is heartbreakingly soft and white against the needle pelt of the water. If she acts polite, they will let her shower as long as she wants.

She fingers the ridges across her thighs, soaps them with her fingertips. He inflicted such wounds. Once, he pushed her and she stumbled and knocked a champagne flute to the ceramic tile. He didn't like when her belly rounded after a big meal, called her "pig" and "beast." He said her ass jiggled and she was too slack for him. He needed tightness. She needed tightness. She wipes that last thought. She will use her time here to shape his details. What he said. What he did. How it could feel.

The guards take her among the other inmates for short periods, to see how she fits in. She does beautifully, supplicating herself but staying tough enough. The other inmates accept her, understand a man like that, the things a woman does that she wouldn't normally do. She listens to their lingo, the real words of spewed hate, the humiliation, degradation, the hands flapping around their heads, the fists, the bruises that don't show. She sees that here is better than any pain there. She sees where she could fit. What she could adapt. She listens and reveals little.

Within a week, she is assigned a cell in 7B with a woman named Ellen Greenwood on trial for running her husband over with a car. She is happy about the move. She could learn a lot from a woman like Ellen Greenwood.

I tried to picture myself visiting her, a knife tucked in my sock, a gun. I would tell her what I thought, what I felt. How she changed me. K had chronic back problems, poor teeth. I had a tailbone that throbbed when I sat upright too long. I would kill Ramona, save the others, set us free, but I couldn't assemble the details. Her face kept getting in the way.

During the cross, I never wavered from my story and got emotional only once more.

"Did you love Ramona Hawkes?" he asked.

"I don't remember." I kept my voice hushed and my gaze distant.

"Is it possible you loved her in February 1986, the day you acted out your play in her basement?"

"I don't remember how I felt."

"Are you attracted to women?"

I knew I should look up, answer with confidence, glare at Ramona. I managed a glance at Witherson's tie. Paisley — probably so he could stain it with impunity.

"Yes. And to men."

"Answer the question put to you, please, Ms. Brown. You and Ramona were attracted to each other, so you made love. Is there anything wrong with that?"

"No, sir, I guess not. Not the way you put it." My head droned and my guts felt hot and soupy. I dug at my ear. Let Cindy put that in the paper.

"Were you jealous of James?"

"Yes."

"Were you attracted to Ramona?"

"Yes."

"Who came up with the idea to act out the hitchhiker kidnapping in the basement?"

"I did." I loathed this man, though it was easy to answer him now. Every piece of nastiness I'd ever hurled at myself had found its way into one of his questions. Here was the true abasement.

"Did you not instigate the events that day, then?"

"Yes, I did."

"Is it not possible, then, that your attraction to Ramona and your jealousy of James were responsible for the events that happened in the Hawkeses' basement that Saturday?"

"Yes, sir." I slumped. "That's one way of looking at it."

A philosopher once said, "The secret of being tiresome is to tell everything," a fair credo for life. What I wanted most from love was to be known — freed from the story, and loved for it, despite it. With Alex it didn't matter if I had to force him to listen to what happened. I needed him to have it inside, and to sit inside it, too. I wanted my story part of the matter around us, what we created, our love. I wanted him to have every excuse to leave. I wanted him to stay.

We got home around three. Alex went for a nap. He invited me but I said no. I needed to start again, to have my morning back, my day. While he slept I took a bubble bath, then, wrapped in towels, watched a new talk show by a former comedienne named Patsy Malone. The episode featured mothers giving their teenage daughters makeovers. One girl, whose breasts and belly rolled out of a snug striped tank-and-tube-skirt ensemble, had a mother in a grey suit with a frilly blouse. *The Patsy Malone Hour* had set the mother up with a thousand dollars and a consultant team. The girl scowled and preened. Her mother fussed. The girl left the stage and they showed cutaways of her haircut, the shopping, the screaming. Throughout, the girl fought to keep her blasé pout. After a commercial break she emerged in a grey suit with a camisole, her flat-ironed hair wispy-fried. Her ankles turned in the heels. She looked broken, airy, placating. Then the mother touched her and she snarled, their love a shining cavity on show for the world. I flipped off the TV.

The air outside had a melting, swooning quality. I scrapped the post office and the Lucky Dollar and instead, sunglasses on, turned the opposite way at the end of Shelby Street. Some gardens had crocuses already, yellow, white, and purple. Some had hyacinths. The intoxicating fumes. Daffodils on the verge. Tulips. Forsythia in full yellow flare.

One day, maybe tonight, maybe weeks from now, months, who knew when, after all the victims had testified, the trial had ended, and Ramona had received her verdict, one day I would hold Alex to his promise. We would play. What we did would be one of many things we did, not the whole of our love, but we'd have it between us then, in the balance, my love equal to his. This picture has stayed with me. This picture, I add to, build, caress. I made the box, I told the story, I wrote it. I have brought Alex into it to make myself real.

I remove strips of wood from the bedroom door frame with a hammer's claw, then thrust the box through with my feet. I squat and get under it with my shoulder to hoist it onto the futon.

Water drips from trees in counterpoint to the clock radio's hum. I plug a 220-volt orange light into an extension cord, switch off the overhead, and haul the light and a roll of resin-coated paper inside my primitive camera.

In the dark, I tape the paper emulsion side out onto the broad end of the box. Then I cover it with a drop cloth. I pull out the lamp cord and stuff the light under the bed then crawl back into the box and fix the door behind me. I rig a wire to pull the cloth away from the photographic paper for the next time the door shuts.

Now I can't leave. The key waits on the outside. I can breathe but not well. My skin feels as if it might tenderize and my flesh slide away from my bones.

I must sleep because I am not aware of when I stop being alone. One moment my mind batters me with escape thoughts and the next he crouches over me. The open door throws the air into porous dusk. He must have felt his way.

He faces me in the mottled dark. Such a vision could appear in a dream.

He holds a soaked cloth against my face until I inhale the acrid chemical. I don't resist. His clothes rustle. He lays his hands on me, and I settle into my ribs' cadence. When he lifts his hands away, my limbs won't move, and the lost sense of air on skin kinks a panic in me that edges the good pain to come.

He switches on the light and drags me by the ankles, then knees, hips, and finally shoulders until I fall dead weight on the mattress. He straightens my head on the pillow and my feet near the bottom, then heaves the box onto the floor where it bashes the dresser and rocks into place, out of reach, weighted side down. The door slams.

The wire is tripped.

The spring-loaded cloth will fall away from the photographic paper. Another, set on a timer, will drop over the perforation after ninety minutes. The low-sensitivity paper negative needs a long exposure to sharpen the image. He lowers his face to mine, his breath in my nostrils, our eyelashes almost touching. The room beyond his eyes ebbs. I detect a glint, hear a ting.

I glance at the discarded escape hatch, the lovers' cradle. Research for my novel was never deep down why I built the box. I made it to hold what was ours, Alex's and mine, to induce Alex to mark my skin and give me the pain that will let me show him the truth of how I love.

He exhales, "I love you," and raises his hand.

acknowledgements

I thank The Canada Council for the Arts for its generous funding and The Helene Wurlitzer Foundation of New Mexico for the gift of time and space.

I thank Julia Noonan and Jill Singleton for guiding me through the Metro West Detention Centre; Dr. Neale Ginsberg and Heather Metcalfe, RN, for information on the medical world; and especially James Cornish, Director of the Special Investigations Unit, for his invaluable and patient insights into matters of policing and the law.

I thank Tess Fragoulis, Daniel Hill, John Miller, and Elizabeth Ruth for their intelligent and encouraging comments; Margaret Hart of the HSW Agency for her faith and zeal; Kirk Howard, Barry Jowett, and the staff at the Dundurn Group for going the next round with me; and Joe Aversa and Pamela Hanft of the Liberal Arts Department at Humber College for their support.

And I thank my friends and family, whose belief in me means worlds.

notes on sources

Tell Everything began with an art installation — American sculptor Ellen Driscoll's *FUGITIVE: The Loophole of Retreat* — and required much research into the worlds of female predators and the Ontario judicial system.

A select list of sources includes Christine Boyle's *The Law of Evidence*; Ray Bull and Rebecca Milne's *Investigative Interviewing Psychology and Practice*; Jim Euale and John Turtle's *Interviewing and Investigation Techniques*; Dr. Robert Hare's *Without Conscience: The Disturbing World of Psychopaths Among Us*; Ann Jones's *Women Who Kill*; The Honourable Fred Kaufman, CM, QC's *Report of the Kaufman Commission on Proceedings Involving Guy Paul Morin*; Melvin Konner's *Becoming a Doctor: A Journal of Initiation in Medical School*; Elliott Layton's *Hunting Humans*; Christine McGuire and Carla Norton's *Perfect Victim*; Patricia Pearson's *When She Was Bad*; Anita Phillips's *A Defence of Masochism*; Wayne Renke's *Evidence: Cases and Materials*; Ann Rule's *The Stranger Beside Me*; Lenore E. Walker's *Battered Woman*; and Stephen Williams's *Invisible Darkness* and *Karla: Pact with the Devil*.

কালমীঢ়

MARQUIS
Marquis Book Printing Inc.

Québec, Canada
2007